INTERNET for KIDS!

A Beginner's Guide to Surfing the Net

NEW UPDATED EDITION!

W9-ALM-537

J0046 PED

Written by Ted Pedersen and Francis Moss

This book is designed primarily for
Windows™-based and Macintosh™ systems.

Where to go online for more cool Internet information:

The Putnam Berkley Group offers a list of books available at:
http://www.readexpress.com

You can write the authors at
kids@internet4kids.com

or visit them online at
http://www.internet4kids.com

DEDICATION

For Phyllis and Phyllis,
and for Caitlin and Zach,
and all the other kids,
no matter what their age,
who'll be riding the Net wave
into the 21st Century.

Editor: Jennifer Repo

Illustrator: Valerie Costantino

Book Designer: Beth Bender

Library of Congress Cataloging-in-Publication Data

Pedersen, Ted.

Internet for kids: a beginner's guide to surfing the Net / written by Ted Pedersen and Francis Moss.

-Rev. ed.

p.   cm.

Summary: Introduces the computer network known as the Internet, providing step-by-step instructions, sample projects, lists of boards to join, and a parents' guide to protect against possible negative aspects of the Internet.

1. Internet (Computer network)—Juvenile literature.

[1. Internet (Computer network) 2. Computers.] I. Moss, Francis.

II. Title.

TK5105.875.I57P43   1997

004.6'7—dc20   97-69816

                                              CIP

                                              AC

ISBN 0-8431-7937-6
First Revised Edition
10 9 8 7 6 5 4 3 2 1

:-) :) :-o :-! :-' :-D :*) :-p (:-& :-" :-(

TABLE OF CONTENTS

Introduction

Do you think of the Internet as a huge, complicated place that only computer experts know about? Is cyberspace a world that you've wanted to explore but didn't know how? Well, think of your computer as your cybership and yourself as the pilot. This book is your pilot's manual to help you learn to navigate through this strange landscape we call the Internet.

Today it seems that everyone is talking about the Net, that magical yellow-brick road winding through cyberspace carrying us into the future. Well, the good news is that it's easy to get there from here. The bad news is that the Internet is like some of the streets in our big cities—full of detours, potholes, and unmarked off-ramps. In other words, there's a lot of interesting

CYBERSPACE

Cyberspace is that place where people and computers meet. It is not a physical place that you can touch or drive to in a car. Think of it as another dimension, beyond outer space but reachable at your fingertips with your computer. The word cyberspace was originally used by a science-fiction writer, William Gibson, and has since become part of our everyday language.

NOTE TO READERS:

Whenever you come across a word you don't understand, just check the Glossary, starting on page 193. If you need to refer back to a particular section of the book where a term is discussed in more detail, check the Index of Terms, starting on page 215.

stuff on the Net, but finding your way around can be difficult.

Searching for a place in cyberspace is like trying to find a house in Tokyo, where each address in a neighborhood is given a number according to when the house was built, rather than where it is on the street. You really need a guide to get around in Tokyo—just like you need a guide to explore, or "surf" the Net.

There are a lot of books about the Internet. Some of them are better than others. But almost none of them has been written for the audience that is going to be most affected by the Internet: You!

That's what this book is all about. It's about piloting your own cybership and traveling at warp speed through an uncharted universe of fun, games, and information—going where no kid has gone before.

Way back in the fall of 1995, we published the first edition of *Internet for Kids*. However, while only a few years have passed since then, generations have passed in Internet time. Everything about the Internet is different than it was, even a year or two ago. That's why we decided that it was time to launch a whole new version of *Internet for Kids*. In the first edition we went into a lot of detail about how to do things on the Internet. Being on the Net was much more complicated in those days. Back then, learning how to navigate cyberspace was like doing long division without a calculator. Today it is simpler to log on to the Internet and start surfing. Now you can navigate the Net simply by putting your computer in "Drive" and letting your cruise-o-matic Web browser do most of the work for you. Well, we think it's not such a bad idea to learn the basics of long division, so we've included the information necessary for you to get online. You may find we've often put in a step or two that may not apply to your situation. If these steps don't apply, simply ignore them and read on!

Now, let's take a brief look at how this book is organized. In the first section of this book, we will walk you through the things you need to know in order to pilot your cybership safely through the Internet. We'll provide instructions on how to get online, what to do once you get there, suggestions about where to go in cyberspace, choosing an online service, and definitions of new and technical terms. Even though cyberspace is always changing, the basics remain the same. And, if you understand the basics, you'll be able to dodge all the glitches and gotchas that might get in your way.

In the special tool-kit section in *Chapter 6: Getting Outfitted (page 95)*, you'll find descriptions of the major Internet service providers, along with their Internet addresses and the programs you may need when you get online. We've also added a *Tech Talk* chapter that will guide you through the technical steps for logging on to the Internet.

Finally, we've updated the *Guide to the Galaxy* with a whole new star system of great places to go and things to see.

So buckle up! We're about to blast off!

Tales of the Internet:

What a Typical Internet Experience Might Be Like

Meet Kate. That's short for Kaitlin. Kate's a red-headed, blue-eyed eighth grader at Hillside Middle School in California.

Kate was just like you a short while ago. She had heard of the **Internet**, but didn't really know much about it. Eager to find out, she read this book from cover to cover. When she finished, she knew everything she needed to know. Now she's a pro!

So if you'd like to see what life on the Internet is like for her now that she knows what it's all about, come join us. We're about to embark on a journey to the world of cyberspace! And don't worry if you don't understand some of the words in this section; they will be explained later on. This chapter is just a little taste of what life is like in cyberspace!

Let's see what a typical day is like for Kate.

It's 3:30 p.m., Monday. Kate arrives home from school, puts her books on her desk in her room, and turns on her computer.

"Ready for takeoff," Kate says to herself as the computer beeps, announcing that it's ready for work.

Phyllis, Kate's mom, comes into her room.

INTERNET

The Internet is simply a network of computers all hooked up together and talking to one another. Once you get on the Internet, you will be able to send electronic mail to your friends—no matter where in the world they live—read bulletin boards, travel in cyberspace on an information superhighway called the Web, and so much more! We'll tell you all about the Internet in this book!

"Hi, hon," she says. "Got homework to do?"

"Yep. A bunch," Kate replies. "A book report for English, and I promised my science teacher I'd look up some stuff about those Mars rocks . . . the ones that might have had organic life in them."

"Sounds like you'll be busy this afternoon," Phyllis says.

"Not only that—I haven't chatted with Elise, my friend in Paris, for a month," Kate says.

"Can I add one more thing to your list?" Kate's mom asks. "I need an idea of what to cook for dinner. I've got broccoli and chicken, and nothing in my cookbook sounds interesting."

"No problem," Kate says as she maneuvers a pointing device, called a **mouse**, attached to her computer.

Kate has a software program that allows her to connect her computer to the Internet. Using her computer, she telephones a bigger computer in her hometown that's connected to still another computer, and so on.

These connected computers, all over the world, make up the Internet.

Kate's computer signals to her that it's connected, or **logged on**, to the Internet. She types in her **password**. Don't look over her shoulder! Her password is hers alone, and she doesn't share it with anyone—not even her best friend, Audrey.

Kate decides first to read the electronic mail messages, or **e-mail**, that other people have sent her. On her computer, she starts a special mail program that finds out if there is any e-mail waiting for her.

As she does this, Kate keeps an eye on the clock. She made an agreement with her parents that her weekday time on the Internet is limited to an hour per day. That way she has time to do other stuff.

Kate finds an e-mail message from a friend she knows only by nickname: Turtle. Turtle lives all the way across the United States in New Jersey. Kate reads the message, smiling at the joke Turtle has written:

> A boy comes up to his father. "Dad, could you do my homework for me?" the boy asks.
>
> His father replies, "Son, I'm surprised you would even ask. You know that it wouldn't be right."
>
> The boy shrugs. "That's okay. After you do it, I'll check it over for mistakes."

As Kate begins to write a reply to Turtle, she glances at the clock again. Because she is allowed only a certain amount of time per day, maybe she ought to wait until tomorrow to reply to Turtle. But then, Kate thinks, her mom probably would agree that hunting recipes and doing homework don't really count against her online time anyway—right? Kate jots down a note to remind herself to talk to her mom about these time-allowed details. She and her mom have agreed to touch base whenever Kate has a question.

Back at her computer again, Kate decides to take care of her mom's request, and begins her search of the Internet for a recipe. She knows that several computers on the Internet have **files** of recipes. She

MOUSE

A mouse is a hand-held device used to move the cursor (the blinking line or arrow that tells you where you are) around the computer screen.

LOG ON

Log on means to connect to a remote computer system. (Log in means the same thing as log on.)

PASSWORD

A password is a secret word that you and only you know. After you enter your user word, you are asked to enter your secret name. That way no one can get on to a network and pretend to be you.

E-MAIL

E-mail stands for electronic mail, which means that it is sent by the computer rather than through your local post office. It's a lot faster than regular mail, too!

FILE

A file is like a folder on your computer that can hold documents, programs, pictures, or other types of computer data.

WEB BROWSER

To get on the Web, you need to run a software program called a Web browser. A Web browser reads documents, displays pictures, plays sounds, and even shows multimedia movie clips. Mosaic was the first Web browser, although Netscape Navigator and Microsoft Internet Explorer are the two most popular Web browsers today.

WORLD WIDE WEB

The World Wide Web, called the Web, is the fastest growing part of the Internet. Part library, supermarket, museum, research tool, idea trove, game room, and art gallery, the Web has rapidly become the most interesting part of the Internet, with millions of locations filled with useful and interesting information.

DISCUSSION GROUP

Discussion groups are people who get together on the Net to talk about a particular topic. On the Internet, there are online discussion groups on everything from aardvarks to zygotes.

uses a program called a **Web browser** to search the **World Wide Web**.

Kate searches for recipes that contain the words "broccoli" and "chicken." Within seconds, she's gotten several recipes. She's also discovered the name of a **discussion group** that publishes hundreds of recipes.

She writes down the name of the discussion group in her Internet log, then instructs her computer to copy the recipes and print them out. After that, Kate runs into the kitchen with the recipe printout.

Phyllis nods as she glances over the recipes. "Thanks, Kate," she tells her daughter. "I'll use one of these recipes tonight and see how it comes out."

Back in her room, Kate wonders whether she should do her homework or chat online with her friend Elise, who lives in France. It's 11:30 p.m. in Paris, where Elise lives. It's pretty late, but Kate has something new she wants to try. With her dad's help, she installed a microphone and new software in her computer. This software will allow Kate to talk with Elise, all the way in Paris, France, over the Internet— for the price of a local telephone call! Elise already has the software and hardware on her machine, and she's been waiting impatiently for Kate to get it. Last week, Elise sent Kate an e-mail message saying she'll wait for her call.

Now Kate runs the software, which makes the connection, computer-to-computer, all the way across the United States to Europe. I hope Elise is still on the Internet, Kate thinks to herself.

On Elise's computer in Paris, a little bell chimes, letting her know she's got a voice telephone call. She quickly slips on a headset and runs the telephone program. A tinny voice comes over the computer's speakers:

"Hello, Elise? This is Kate."

"Bonjour, ma chère," Elise begins.

We won't listen in. Instead, let's drop by Grant Elementary School, where Kate's little brother, Zack, is working after school in the computer lab.

Although younger than his sister—he's eleven—Zack shares Kate's blue eyes and freckles, as well as her love of computers. He's pretty good at this computer stuff, too. Their father, Frank, is a plumber who got both of his children interested in computers when he started using one to keep track of his customers, his suppliers, and his bills.

Zack remembers that when he and Kate were younger, they would sit with their father while he worked on the computer. When Frank was finished with his work, he'd load up a computer game they all could play.

Now Zack stays after school in the computer lab twice a week to help his teacher keep the lab organized and get the computers ready for the next day's classes. In return, his teacher lets Zack spend some time surfing the Internet.

Today Zack has some homework to do, too. His class just finished reading *Tom Sawyer*, by Mark Twain, and Zack has to write a report about the author. But his school library doesn't have the books he needs for researching life on the Mississippi River during Tom Sawyer's time. Zack thinks that the main branch of his local library might have the books, but the staff there is often too busy to look up the books for him.

But just recently the library put its card catalog online, so Zack can find out not only if the library has the books he's looking for, but whether or not they're checked out.

Zack connects his school's computer to the library's computerized card catalog. He sees that his library has two copies of one of the books he's looking for, and one of them is on the shelf. He makes a mental note to stop by on the way home from school and check out the book.

Zack thinks that if he had more time he could find lots of information on his topic online. In just a few years, the Internet has become a huge "virtual library," with hundreds of thousands of books, articles, and essays available at the click of a mouse. But Zack knows that searching the Net can take time, and he has some other cool stuff to do online.

Back at home, Kate looks at her clock. It's now 4:30. She decides to finish her homework, and to do this, she must search online for some key information.

Kate logs on to a Web **search site** and types in the phrase "*Mars rocks.*" The site returns a list of possible sources of information.

She clicks on an underlined (or highlighted) phrase, called a **hypertext link**, and is instantly connected with a computer at the Lake Afton Public Observatory in Kansas. It has loads of pictures and information about Mars rocks. Imagine! Kate doesn't even have to leave her room!

She picks three **digitized** images of the rocks, and one image of the area where the rocks were found, along with an article about them, and proceeds to copy them onto her computer.

Then she prints them out on her color printer. She smiles because she knows this will definitely get her some points with her teacher!

SEARCH SITE

A search site is a location in cyberspace where you can enter words or phrases to search for information.

HYPERTEXT LINK

A hypertext link is specially formatted text (usually highlighted or underlined) that will allow you to jump to the Web page that the hypertext is connected to. That new page will very likely have a hypertext link to take you back to your starting point.

DIGITIZED

Pictures or sounds are digitized, or processed, into bits and bytes so they can be transmitted over phone lines and viewed on your computer.

ICONS

Icons are pictures that represent the program or type of function in the software. For example, a picture of a printer means "click here" to print, and a picture of a disk means "click here" to save your work.

Just then her mom peeks in the room. "Can you tell Zack to come home?" she asks Kate.

"Sure, Mom." Kate opens up her e-mail program and starts to type.

Back at Grant School, Zack is doing his favorite online activity—playing a MUD. That stands for Multiple User Dimensions. MUDs are role-playing games that exist on the Internet for entertainment purposes, and what's really great is that many players, on computers anywhere in the world, can all play at the same time.

Zack is playing a MUD started by kids his own age! He follows the instructions and soon he's presented with a three-dimensional world containing several avatars, which are **icons** that represent other players in the game. Zack finds his favorite avatar, a sea horse, and moves it into the playing field. Other players have chosen knights in armor, rabbits, or human heads as their avatars.

The object of this game is to solve several puzzles before the other players can. Some players might team up with him; others might be in competition with him. Zack must answer questions about his location and find secrets hidden in the playing arena in order to continue. As he moves forward, 3-D images of buildings, streets, vehicles, and other figures appear to flow past him on either side, just as if he were actually moving in this cyberspace world.

Zack moves his sea horse avatar to a building, where a chess piece with a girl's face on it confronts him. Is she a friend or an enemy?

Before Zack can decide, his e-mail program beeps, letting him know that he has mail waiting. Zack pauses his game, then reads the message. It's from his sister, Kate:

"Time to come home for dinner, little brother."

With a sigh, Zack quits the game and logs off the Internet. He waves good-bye to his teacher as he heads for home. He hates to end an adventure in cyberspace so early. Wouldn't you? If you knew what you were missing, you sure would!

Zack and Kate seem like real Internet pros, don't they? Well, they weren't always. Once, not so very long ago, they were beginners, just like you. Let's travel back in time and see how Zack and Kate learned about the Internet.

PART I

Cadet:

Welcome to Cyberspace Academy

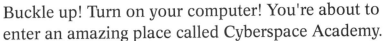

SCROLLING

When you can't see the entire document or picture on your computer monitor, you can use the mouse or arrow keys to scroll, or move the screen up, down, or sideways.

Buckle up! Turn on your computer! You're about to enter an amazing place called Cyberspace Academy.

Cyberspace Academy is a place for learning and playing, talking and seeing, inventing and interacting.

Where is Cyberspace Academy? It exists only in this book, but it's the place you'll go, just like Kate and Zack, to learn all about the Internet.

Are you ready, Cadet? Let's go! Tighten your safety belts as we follow Kate and Zack on their amazing adventures at Cyberspace Academy.

Kate and Zack stare at the message **scrolling** across their computer screen:

File	Edit	View

CONGRATULATIONS!

You have been accepted into Cyberspace Academy.

"Wow!" Zack says. "This is great. When do we pack?"

"We don't," Kate reminds her little brother. "This is the computer age. We don't have to go to the Academy. It comes to us online, through the computer."

On the screen the message continues:

Your mission as Cyberspace Cadets is to graduate with enough training so you can pilot your personal computer safely through the Internet, to search out information that will help you learn new things, and to discover new friends who are also surfing the Net on similar missions.

"So when do we begin?" asks Zack, who is anxious to get started. Kate has to admit that she is as excited as her brother.

"You begin right now," says a voice from inside

their computer. There, in a corner of the screen, Zack and Kate see a cool-looking guy in a Cyberspace Academy uniform with sergeant's stripes on his collar. "I'm your guide through basic training, First Sergeant Abraham Lincoln Kennedy. But you can call me CyberSarge. So, what're you kids waiting for? Let's get started on your first assignment!"

Both Kate and Zack are nervous. It's one thing to read about the Internet in books and magazines or to hear about it on TV, but this is real thing. They are about to plug into the digital generation. They are about to become real **Internauts**.

"Don't sweat it, kids," says CyberSarge. "You may be just **newbies** now, but come graduation day, both of you will be navigating the Net like pros. I guarantee it."

"What's a newbie?" asks Kate.

"Glad you asked," says CyberSarge. "There are a lot of new words you'll be hearing during your training. If you look along the side of your computer screen, you'll see an open book with a little bookworm perched on top. Whenever there's a new word—what I like to call **geek speak**—then the bookworm will tell you what that word means."

CyberSarge points to the side of the screen, where the bookworm explains the new word he has just used.

"Being a **geek** sounds like fun," says Zack.

"It can be," agrees CyberSarge. "But geeks often spend too much time at their computers, surfing the Net, and playing games. They forget about doing their chores around the house and finishing their homework. Sometimes they even ignore their family and friends."

"I'd never do that," promises Kate. "Now, what's a newbie?"

WHO IS CYBERSARGE?

CyberSarge, like Cyberspace Academy, exists only in this book. He's a helpful friend who will lead Kate, Zack, and you through the maze we call the Internet. Listen and learn from CyberSarge and soon you'll be surfing the Net like a real pro!

INTERNAUTS

We call the people who explore outer space "astronauts." So it's only natural to call those who travel through cyberspace "Internauts."

GEEK SPEAK

Geek speak refers to words that are usually only used in reference to computers and being on the Internet.

GEEKS

Geeks are people who are really excited about computers and are proud of it.

CYBERSARGE SAYS:

We're all new here in cyberspace. When you become an expert, remember how you felt your first day online and treat other newbies the way you would have wanted to be treated.

NEWBIE

A newbie is someone who logs on to the Internet for the first time, someone who's just learning his or her way around. There's nothing wrong with being a newbie. We all are newbies whenever we try to do something new.

"That's us," says Zack. "We're newbies."

"So what do we learn first?" asks Kate, who doesn't want to remain a newbie one minute longer than she has to.

"Well, the best place to start is to learn a little bit about where the Internet came from and what it is today." CyberSarge steps aside to let the kids' first lesson scroll across the computer screen:

File	Edit	View

A SHORT HISTORY OF THE INTERNET

Once upon a time, way back in 1969, people in colleges and governments were learning how to use computers to solve problems. But even though they used simple word processors to write down what they learned and store it in their computers, there were no daily updated libraries where people could go to read what others had just written and make suggestions.

So someone who worked for the government in an agency called the Defense Advanced Research Projects Agency (DARPA) came up with the idea that several computers could be linked together by wires so they could "talk" to one another. A note that was written on one computer could be sent immediately to all the other computers that were connected to it. The people at the agency called that group of four computers a **network**.

The network's name was DARPANET, after the first letters in the name: Defense Advanced Research Projects Agency with NET (meaning network here, not Internet) added to the end.

The network was a great idea and it quickly grew, but the name was shortened by dropping the "D" and calling it simply ARPANET.

ARPANET grew and grew over time, and more and more computers were added over phone wires. In 1983, the military research people thought they would be better off having their own private network, so they created the MILNET network.

Then, in 1984, another government agency, the National Science Foundation, started the NSFNET network, which linked together five **supercomputer** centers and made the information available to any school that needed it.

That is, everyone who entered a network was connected to at least one of the supercomputer centers, and that gave them access to all the other computers on the network—even to those places that were hooked into the network through another **gateway**.

Think of gateways as telephone switchboards. When you use the telephone to call anyone else who has a telephone, the switchboard makes sure each call gets connected. For instance, to call across the country, you have to go through several switchboards to get there. This idea of connecting all the switchboards together is called networking.

The NSFNET network became very popular. More computers and more wires had to be added because everyone in schools and government wanted to get on to the network. Instead of just adding more computers to the first network of supercomputers, they added more networks and wired all the networks together. They called all these interconnected networks an Inter-Net-Network.

Today we call it the Internet.

Because lots of people by now have their own personal computers, the Internet has become even more popular.

DID YOU KNOW THAT?

Someone logs on to the Internet for the first time every 1.6 seconds.

NETWORK

A network is simply a group of computers joined together so they can communicate with one another. A network can be as small as two computers joined together by wires in an office, or as large as millions of computers spread all over the world and joined by telephone lines, satellite relays, fiber-optic cables, or radio links.

SUPERCOMPUTER

This is a mainframe-sized computer that operates much faster than a normal desktop or laptop computer, and is used for special science and military projects.

GATEWAY

A gateway is a computer system that acts as a translator between different types of computers to allow them to interact in cyberspace.

In the last ten years it has grown from about 5,000 users to more than 50 million. And more than a million new users go **online** every month.

"Wow!" Kate is amazed. "That's a lot of users."

"And a lot of wires," Zack adds.

"In the old days, when your parents were kids, phone lines hooked the networks together all over the country," CyberSarge says. "Now the connections are made mainly by **fiber-optic** cables that are much smaller and carry a lot more information a lot faster—and by satellites. Today, the whole world is linked together by the Internet."

"The whole world . . ." Kate's eyes light up as she imagines all the places she'll be able to visit and all the new friends she will make. "This is going to be so fun!"

"It will be," CyberSarge promises. "But before you two go leaping out into cyberspace on your own, you need some surfing lessons."

"We're ready!" Kate and Zack reply in unison.

ONLINE

When you go online, it simply means your computer is hooked to another computer over the phone lines.

FIBER OPTIC

Fiber optics are high-speed cables that are much smaller than the old wire cables used for telephone lines. They can carry much more information at much faster speeds. Most long-distance phone traffic is carried through high-volume fiber-optic cables.

Chapter 1

Life on the Internet:

What's It All About?

It is the morning after Kate and Zack have started attending Cyberspace Academy. It also happens to be Saturday, so there's no school. After breakfast, they seat themselves in front of their computer terminal, anxious to get started. Kate **boots up** the computer, and a few seconds later, CyberSarge appears on the screen.

"Ready to blast off!" Zack exclaims enthusiastically.

BOOT UP

You do this when you start up your computer by turning on the power.

19

CyberSarge smiles. He knows that kids today are eager to try new things on their computers. "Okay," he says. "Strap in and hang on tight. Next stop—cyberspace!"

Kate holds her mouse tightly in her hand. This is exciting. "What do I do?" she asks.

"Today, you two can just sit back and leave the driving to an old-timer—namely me," says CyberSarge. "I'm going to take you on a short guided tour of the Internet so you'll get the lay of the land. Then, in the next sessions, we'll go through each part of the Internet in detail. But for now just enjoy."

The kids watch as their next lesson scrolls across the screen:

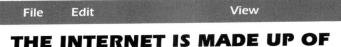

| File | Edit | View |

THE INTERNET IS MADE UP OF A LOT OF DIFFERENT PARTS

The Internet is not just one thing, but a lot of different pieces that fit together.

1. WORLD WIDE WEB

The World Wide Web first went online in 1992 and is the fastest-growing and most popular piece of the Internet. When you're on the Web you can see pictures, listen to sounds, and jump almost instantly from one Web page to another, even if that means traveling to the other side of the world.

Being on the Web means that you can visit anywhere in the world, just as if you were really there. You may experience everything from being part of a river rafting expedition in Africa to working alongside astronauts on a space-shuttle mission.

2. E-MAIL

E-mail is the oldest part of the Internet. The first e-mail letter was sent from a computer at the University of California, Los Angeles, in the early 1970s. E-mail (remember, the "e" stands for electronic) is simply a way to write a letter on one computer and then send it to another computer, where it can be read. Although today's e-mail programs are much more sophisticated than the first ones, the basic concept remains the same.

Just think: You can e-mail a note to your friends who live just down the street, or to those thousands of miles away. The best part is that the letters arrive in their **electronic mailboxes** almost instantly!

3. USENET NEWSGROUPS

Usenet newsgroups are part of a huge bulletin-board system. People all over the world can read and post messages on thousands of topics. For example, if you're a fan of a particular music group, there's probably a newsgroup devoted to them where you can exchange news about the band's latest tour, swap publicity photos, gossip, or just compare favorite songs with other kids—and grown-ups—all over the world.

4. CHAT

Chat, which is also known as IRC, or Internet Relay Chat, has become a very popular Internet service. Online chat rooms are like meeting halls where a bunch of people can get together and talk. In a chat room, you can have a group discussion with kids who live in different cities. Chatting via the Internet is great because people can talk without leaving their homes.

5. FTP

FTP stands for File Transfer Protocol. FTP allows computers all over the world to exchange files with one another. Whenever you **download** a software program

ELECTRONIC MAILBOX

An electronic mailbox is the place where your cyberspace mail goes. When you sign up with an Internet provider, the software you receive will include e-mail capabilities and your own mailbox. It is the cyberspace version of your mailbox at home.

USENET NEWSGROUPS

Usenet newsgroups are online groups in which you can discuss almost any subject you can imagine—from how to house-train your pet to what the latest UFO rumor is.

DOWNLOAD

When you download, you are receiving information in your computer from another computer, usually through a modem.

or the latest game from Boston, Massachusetts, or Bangkok, Thailand, you're using FTP.

6. GOPHER

Gopher was created as a way to find information stored in computers around the world. An interactive menu system—allowing you to select the information you want—made searching throughout "Gopherspace" for key words and phrases easy. It was, in many ways, the forerunner to the World Wide Web. Gopher was developed at the University of Minnesota in 1991 and took its name from the University's mascot, the Golden Gopher. Gopher is used to search for documents that are stored on various computers, mostly at universities and libraries. There are hundreds of thousands of books, articles, and research papers that Gopher can locate so you can read them right on your own computer.

While Gopher isn't as glamorous as the World Wide Web, it's a wonderful library that can help you with your homework.

"It doesn't seem like the Internet is very old," Kate says.

"It isn't," CyberSarge replies. "Parts of it, like Gopher and the World Wide Web, are younger than you are."

"That means we're pioneers exploring new frontiers." Kate likes that idea.

"Okay," interrupts Zack, "there are lots of things on the Internet. But what good are they to us?"

"I'm glad you asked," replies CyberSarge. The kids watch as their next lesson scrolls on the screen:

File   Edit   View

WHAT YOU CAN DO ON THE INTERNET

It's nice to know that the Internet is there, but why would you want to go there?

The simple answer is that the Internet—like our computers—is a tool that can help us grow smarter.

Think of your computer as a "brain machine" that helps you do things with your mind, just as a hammer and screwdriver help you do things with your hands.

Now, think of the Internet as "brain food" that lets you imagine new things and visit exciting new places. A century ago, most people hardly ever left their own neighborhoods. The world beyond their own hometown was as strange as the dark side of the moon.

Today, the Internet has opened up the whole world to us. Instead of a neighborhood, we have an exciting new cyberhood!

People often say that we live in an "information society," where "the more you know, the more you grow."

Well, the Internet can help you grow smarter in five basic ways:

1. COMMUNICATING

With e-mail and chat groups you can talk to kids and grown-ups all over the world. You might find a new key pal in Paris. (Key pals are pen pals that you talk to through the computer.) You might talk to an archaeologist who's digging up dinosaur bones in China's Gobi Desert. By talking and listening you are meeting people from different places who are doing really exciting things. On the Internet your neighborhood is the whole world.

DID YOU KNOW THAT?

The Internet population has been doubling every year. There are 50 million users online today, and more than 1 million of them are kids.

2. EXPLORING

The Internet connects you to the rest of the world and

lets you explore other places and learn new things while sitting at your computer. You can become a **virtual tourist**, visiting other cities and countries online without having to physically go there! You can actually tour the famous museums of Europe, or even go to the planets and moons in our solar system. Wherever you want to go, you can go there on the Internet.

3. FINDING

Everything is connected to everything else on the

Internet. Start anywhere, and if you search hard enough, you can find almost anything, whether it's the definition of a word, a little-known historical fact for your homework assignment, or a new recipe for a Saturday night party. Whatever you're looking for, chances are you can find it somewhere on the Internet. And when you become full-fledged Internauts, you'll know how to conduct searches to find what you're looking for.

4. LEARNING

There are two ways you'll learn while surfing the Net.

One way is by searching for something you want to know about, like who invented the bicycle. The other is by finding something new and unexpected by accident. That's called

"serendipity." Serendipitous learning, or learning through serendipity, happens all the time on the Internet. That's part of the fun of being online. You never know what you might come across!

5. PLAYING

Have you ever heard the saying, "All work and no play makes for dull boys and girls?" Having fun and playing games can stretch our imaginations. Playing opens up new ways of looking at the world. And there are lots of ways to play on the Internet.

"We'll take a closer look at each one of these in turn," CyberSarge says as he pops up on the computer screen. "Let's start with *communicating*."

"I know e-mail is sending letters and chatting is like using the telephone, only you talk with your keyboard rather than with your mouth," says Kate.

"And there's even **telephony**," Zack adds. "I've heard it turns your computer into a real telephone."

"That's right. Voice and even video communication are becoming more popular on the Internet every day," says CyberSarge. "You will need powerful computers to use those. But slower computers still can send and receive e-mail."

"I have a deaf friend," says Kate. "Sometimes I write things down on a notepad so she'll understand."

"That's one of the nice things about the Internet," says CyberSarge. "It doesn't matter who you are or what you look like. People will know you only by what you type in to express yourself."

VIRTUAL TOURIST

Being a virtual tourist simply means visiting places in cyberspace without having to physically go there. You go there online and in your imagination.

TELEPHONY

Telephony is the combination of the Internet with the telephone, which gives you the ability to talk long distance over the Internet. This is like a personal phone call, but you use the computer.

"I like that," says Kate. "You can really make friends and get to know someone without worrying about how you look or the clothes you wear."

"That's the good news about the Internet," says CyberSarge.

"So what's the bad news?" wonders Zack.

"The bad news about the Internet is that a few people take advantage of it. There aren't many of them, but, like a bad apple, they try to spoil things for the rest of us. They hide themselves in disguises—like wearing Halloween costumes—and you're not always sure who they really are."

"So what do we do about that?" asks Kate.

"The same thing you do when you answer the telephone and you don't know who you're talking to," replies CyberSarge. "Don't answer personal questions about yourself or your home. The Internet is kind of like the old telephone system."

"How's that?" Zack asks.

"In the old days people used party lines, which meant that you could call up a phone number that a lot of other people were already talking on, and all those other people could hear what you were saying on the phone. It's that way on the Internet. Other people might be listening in. The most important thing to remember is: Don't say anything on the Internet that you wouldn't want to say out loud in public. And never, ever give out your full name, your address, or your home phone number. Always play it safe."

"We'll definitely remember those rules," Kate promises.

"Good!" says CyberSarge with a big smile. "Now let's take a closer look at how we *communicate* on the Internet."

File	Edit	View

COMMUNICATING ON THE INTERNET

E-mail is the most common way to communicate on the Internet. We do it by writing a letter, sending it to someone, and then getting a reply. Even if you're not a great letter writer, exchanging "e-notes" with your friends can be a lot of fun. You can send jokes and even attach pictures to be downloaded.

E-mail works just like snail mail, which is what Internauts call the regular mail that the post office delivers to your house. The big difference is that e-mail is delivered in cyberspace.

Chatting is another way to communicate, but in **real time**. You call up people through the Internet and "talk" to them the way you do on the phone, only you're writing and reading on your computer rather than talking and listening with a phone in your hand.

Sometimes you chat with just one person, but there are also **chat groups** where several people can talk. Chat groups can be a little confusing because several people may try to talk at one time. We'll discuss some helpful rules for chatting in *Chapter 8: Tech Talk (page 161).*

Telephony is the newest way to chat. It is the merging of the telephone with the Internet that allows you to talk long distance through your local Internet connection. If you have a microphone on your computer, you can talk into it as you would a telephone. Actually telephony works more like a walkie-talkie. Telephony is kind of like a personal phone call because you are talking with just one person, whereas voice chat means you are talking with a lot of people.

Mailing lists and newsgroups are two more ways of communicating. You subscribe to them just as you would

REAL TIME
When you do something in real time, it means you're doing it right now. It's live and online.

CHAT GROUPS
Chat groups are online addresses where many people talk to each other at once.

subscribe to a favorite magazine. Some of these groups have hundreds of subscribers. When you write a letter to a group, everyone on the list gets a copy of your letter. And you get a copy in your e-mail mailbox of every letter sent by the other subscribers.

Mailing lists are regulated by a Majordomo or **Listserver**, a special program that automatically sorts the incoming messages and then sends them out to all the current list subscribers. That can be a lot of letters, so be careful about how many lists you subscribe to—or you may end up with a hundred new letters every day.

Usenet newsgroups are similar to mailing lists, but instead of receiving hundreds of e-mail letters, you get a list of **headers** from the articles that have been posted since the last time you checked. This way you can choose to read only those articles that interest you. You can also follow a particular **thread** without having to read all the other articles. You might think of newsgroups as bulletin boards, where people tack up new notes and reply to old ones.

LISTSERVER

A Listserver is a special program that handles e-mail among subscribers to a mailing list or a discussion group.

HEADERS

A header is a phrase at the beginning of a message that tells you what the message is going to be about, such as "My Favorite Movies."

THREADS

Threads are discussions within a newsgroup. All of the replies to a particular message make up a thread. They are linked together by the mail server. For example, perhaps you've subscribed to a newsgroup about pets, but you want to read and reply to only the threads about dogs. All of the messages about dogs are grouped together in a thread, so they're easy to find.

"E-mail sounds great!" exclaims Kate. She is thinking about all the key pals she can write to—even her friend Julie who moved to Florida.

"E-mail is still the most popular way to use the Internet," says CyberSarge.

"But what if I don't write so well?" asks Zack, who can remember writing only two letters in his whole life.

"Don't worry, it's something you'll learn quickly," replies CyberSarge. "That's another good thing about the Internet and e-mail: It forces us to think about what we're going to say and to say it simply. Short and sweet is the rule for e-mail."

"Sometimes it's hard to say what you mean using just words," says Kate. She often uses a lot of facial expressions and hand gestures to punctuate her speech when she gets into a really serious discussion.

"That's what smileys are for," says CyberSarge.

"What's a smiley?" ask Kate and Zack together.

CyberSarge smiles and points to the computer screen, where the kids see:

CYBERSARGE SAYS:

Mailing lists will often let you subscribe to a digest, which is a single e-mail message listing the subjects (and sometimes brief summaries) of all the daily letters.

| File | Edit | View |

SMILEYS AND ACRONYMS

When you're face-to-face with someone, you can smile, frown, or make a whole bunch of facial expressions to help emphasize your words. Smileys can show someone that you're happy, sad, angry, or just plain bored when you're on the computer. In e-mail, your words have to carry your thoughts by themselves, so people invented smileys to punctuate their phrases.

There are two basic types of smileys: Those with pictures and those with words.

The picture smileys are made up of different combinations of punctuation marks. Look at them sideways to get the idea. They include:

:-)	smile with a nose
:)	smile without a nose
:*)	just clowning around
:-D	said with a smile
:-!	you put your foot in your mouth
:-]	said with a smirk
:/)	it's not funny
:-"	said pursing your lips
:-r	sticking out your tongue
(:-&	you're angry
:-o	you're shouting
:-@	you're SCREAMING
:-(	you're unhappy
:-c	you're really unhappy
||*(	offering a handshake
||*)	accepting a handshake
[]	giving a hug
:-x	giving a kiss
@>->-	offering a rose

:-*   oops!

'-)   said with a wink

Some of the word smileys, which are always bracketed between < and >, include:

<grin> or just plain <g>

<frown>

<chuckle>

<smile>

<smirk> or a <wink>

even a <silly grin>

<grin>

Other smileys made with words are called acronyms. They are also shortcuts you can use to express yourself when you're on the computer. It's like writing "OK" instead of "okay," or "BTW" to stand for "by the way." Some common acronyms are:

ADN	any day now
BBS	bulletin board system
BRB	be right back
CU	see you
CUL	see you later
DTRT	do the right thing
FAQ	frequently asked question
FYI	for your information
GAL	get a life
GIGO	garbage in, garbage out. (This is a popular computer term, meaning that a computer will produce wrong information if it's given flawed data.)
IMO	in my opinion
IMHO	in my humble opinion
LOL	laughing out loud
POV	point of view
ROTFL	rolling on the floor laughing
RPG	role-playing games

LOL

SYSOP	SYStem OPerator
TGIF	thank God it's Friday
TIA	thanks in advance

"Cool!" says Zack. "I can even make up my own acronyms—like WTFS: Watch That First Step."

"Exactly!" CyberSarge confirms. "And when you invent an acronym, you just type it out in capital letters and then type out what it means. Who knows, people might like it enough to start using it."

"Great," comments Kate. "Now what do we do next?"

"The next major reason for being on the Internet is to be an explorer," says CyberSarge.

"That's me," says Zack. "I love to explore and go where no kid has gone before."

"Exploring on the Internet is like discovering a new galaxy. You'll find all kinds of new places to visit, learn new things, and meet new friends. And because there are hundreds of new Web sites coming

online every day, you'll never have enough time to visit all the places there are."

"How many places are there?" asks Kate.

"There are approximately 30 million home pages on the World Wide Web."

"Home pages?" asks Kate, with a puzzled look on her face.

"What are they?" asks Zack.

"One thing at a time, guys," says CyberSarge.

File   Edit   View

EXPLORING ON THE NET

THE WORLD WIDE WEB

The World Wide Web—more commonly called the Web or just the WWW—is young and still growing, but it has quickly become the most important part of the Internet.

The Web was invented by Tim Berners-Lee of CERN, the European Laboratory for Particle Physics, in Geneva, Switzerland. It made its first public appearance on the Internet in 1992 and was an immediate smash hit. By the end of 1993 there were more than 200 **Web servers** up and running.

The number of **Web sites** online is growing every second. It's growing so fast, no one is really sure how many Web sites there are. But everyone agrees that the number is in the millions.

The Web has pictures and **hypertext**, which allows you to "jump" from one place to another, all over the world, with a single click of a mouse.

The advantage of using hypertext is that you can get more information about a particular subject by clicking on a hypertext link with your mouse. If you don't know what the word means, you can click on that word and a definition will pop up.

Documents can also be linked to other documents by completely different authors—much like the footnotes in your textbooks at school. But instead of having to turn to another chapter or get another book, you click on the highlighted or underlined words (hypertext links) to reach a related document instantly. In short, a hypertext document will have highlighted words or icons on the page that are linked to other documents.

WEB SERVER
A Web server is a computer attached to a network that is used for communication with the World Wide Web.

WEB SITES
A Web site is a place on the World Wide Web that has a unique address, like a house that you can visit. When you visit a Web site, the first page you see is called the home page. Just as a house is made up of rooms, a Web site is made up of pages.

HYPERTEXT
Hypertext was invented in 1965 by Ted Nelson. It lets you move easily from Web site to Web site or from page to page. For example, if you were reading a history book about the Civil War, you might click on a highlighted or underlined word, which means that information is "linked" to other related information, such as a map of the place you were reading about.

"Okay," says Kate, "I'm beginning to understand the Web. But what's a home page?"

"A home page is like the table of contents page or the front page of a magazine," explains CyberSarge. "It's where you start. Every Web site has a home page, which might be its only page. But most often the home page will let you click on highlighted words and icons that will lead you to other pages. Let's say a big company wants to set up a Web site. But maybe not all the information about the company can fit on one page. So, the home page serves as the introductory page, and there might be many more pages linked to the home page. Other Web sites might have *only* a home page."

"The Web sounds like a great place to explore!" says Zack.

"The Internet is so big," says Kate. "Looking for what you want must be like panning for gold. How do you find the nuggets in all that information?"

"It can be confusing. Think of the Internet as a huge information library." CyberSarge frowns, then continues. "Unfortunately, the information on the Internet isn't always labeled as clearly or organized as well as books are in a library."

"I need to know about Thomas Jefferson for my homework assignment," Kate says. "Where would I start looking?"

"Later on we'll take a closer look at some of the specific **search engines** you can use. But for now let's learn about two basic ways you can search the Internet," answers CyberSarge.

SEARCH ENGINES

Search engines were created because the Web is so big and it can be confusing if you're trying to find something specific. A search engine works like the librarian in your school library. You tell the librarian what you're looking for, and he or she will point to the books where you might find the information.

File	Edit	View

FINDING IT ON THE INTERNET

The Internet contains thousands of places and millions of documents. Finding what you want can be difficult and take a very long time if you don't narrow down your search. You'll want to go to the places that are most likely to contain the information you're looking for. One place to start might be at a Web site such as Yahoo, which contains a list of thousands of other Web sites that you search for by category.

Fortunately, these sites are broken down by categories so that you can find those that deal with astronomy or medicine, or whatever subject you're looking for.

Once you find a site that has information about your subject, you'll be able to click on links that will take you to other sites covering the same subject.

The other way to search the Internet is to use a search engine to look for **key words**.

To find something on the Net, it's important to know just what you are looking for and to select the key words that will get you there.

CYBERSARGE SAYS:

Think of key words as markers that point to the locations of information on the World Wide Web. A key word might be a subject word such as "sports," or a group of words contained in a document, such as "Civil War cavalry."

"Exploring and finding are really about learning," concludes CyberSarge.

"It sounds like too much fun to be learning," Zack says with a smile.

CyberSarge smiles back. "Learning is supposed to be fun. Think about the things you know the most about."

"Softball and astronomy are my best subjects," says Kate without hesitation.

"That's because you enjoy reading about them and doing them. The really good thing about the Internet is that it can make things that you're not excited

VIRTUAL REALITY

Virtual reality, or VR, is a world that exists only at a VR arcade or in cyberspace. To experience today's virtual reality in an arcade, you put on a special helmet or glasses, gloves, and a bodysuit. These are connected to VR devices through a computer in the arcade. When you walk, move, speak, smell, hear, or touch something, it seems as if you are actually inside the imaginary world. To experience today's virtual reality in cyberspace, you put glasses on and, using gloves or your mouse, you connect to a VR site in cyberspace. Once online, you can walk around that virtual world just like you would walk around in a mall arcade.

MULTIMEDIA

The combination of images, sound, and motion, which is built into many of today's computer games. Most often found on **CD-ROMs**, multimedia games are beginning to be seen on the World Wide Web.

CD-ROM

CD-ROM stands from "Compact Disk-Read Only Memory." The most popular high-capacity disk drive for computers, a CD-ROM drive can store more than 600 megabytes of data. Even an entire encyclopedia collection can be stored!

about much more interesting. You'll be learning new things all the time on the Internet. And this brings us to our next lesson," says CyberSarge.

File	Edit	View

LEARNING ON THE INTERNET

While it could be said that everything you do is a learning experience, there are specific ways in which the Internet can be an educational tool and can help you with your schoolwork.

There are several Web sites that can help answer your questions when you have homework problems. You can visit libraries, schools, and other Web sites that are filled with information on almost every subject you can imagine. And you should also check the newsgroups that deal with your subject area.

"Okay, we've covered communicating, exploring, finding, and learning. That leaves playing!" Zack says eagerly.

"The Internet is full of games," says CyberSarge. "Just a short while ago, all Internet games were played with text only, which was kind of like listening to old radio shows: You had to imagine what everything looked like. Now there are three-dimensional worlds you can "wander" around in. You can even play online games with other kids all over the world."

File	Edit	View

PLAYING ON THE NET

Whether you're into text-based games or want to play in an interactive three-dimensional environment against other players, there's something on the Internet for you.

MUDs were the first multi-player games on the Internet. They are online **virtual reality** worlds that are built from words and you picture them in your imagination.

MUDs quickly became very popular on college campuses all around the world. Multiple User Dimension games, which is what MUD stands for, are electronic games and adventures that run on a large network, usually by university computers.

Players will often spend hours logged on to fantasy worlds based on science fiction stories or popular novels about dragons and wizards.

Since the original MUD was created, hundreds of MUD games have cropped up around the world. Now, with the development of multimedia capabilities on the Net, new three-dimensional virtual reality worlds have started to come online. In these imaginary worlds, people can "wander" through alien landscapes, interact with others, and play games in exciting video arcade-like environments.

Multimedia—the combined use of text, graphics, video, and sound—is becoming very important on the Net, and will be even more important in the future when there are faster modems.

"I can't wait to play an online game!" says an impatient Zack.

"They can be fun and entertaining," agrees CyberSarge. "But like anything you enjoy, you have to be careful not to overdo it. Right now it's time to stop for the day. Tomorrow we'll actually go online!

Chapter 2
Preparing for Lift-off:
How Do I Get Online?

CyberSarge is waiting for Kate and Zack the next morning when they turn on their computer and sit down in front of the screen. This is the big day. Today they are logging on to the Internet for real.

"I have one question before we start," says Kate.

"Ask away," replies CyberSarge.

"Well, we have a PC computer with Windows. But my friend Lisa has a Macintosh. Can we both get on to the Internet?"

"Absolutely. There is software for both Windows and Mac systems. Almost all the online services, like CompuServe, Prodigy, and America Online, support both types of systems. So do the popular Internet software programs such as Netscape Navigator, used for browsing the World Wide Web, and Eudora, used for e-mail."

"What are we waiting for?" prompts Zack, anxious to get started.

"Well, the first thing we need to do is get a gateway on to the Internet."

"What's a gateway, again?"

"Remember how all the computers on the Internet are connected to one another? Well, we need to connect to one of those computers. That computer system we connect to is known as our Internet service provider, or ISP. That service provider is our gateway to the Net."

CyberSarge steps aside so the kids can read the lesson on the screen:

File	Edit	View

HOW DO I GET ONLINE?

There are two ways for you to access the Internet through your personal computer or your Macintosh:

1. COMMERCIAL SERVICES

The most popular national commercial online services, such as America Online, Prodigy, Microsoft Network, and CompuServe, all have gateways on to the Internet. These services can provide a good way for you to start surfing the Net since they have simple icons that make it easy to get help when you're online. You also have access to their special services, including e-mail. The downside is that you may be limited to using their software, so if you have a great e-mail program that isn't part of your online service, you won't be able to use it.

The cost for each of these varies; however, most commercial services now have unlimited usage for about twenty dollars per month.

2. INTERNET SERVICE PROVIDER (ISP)

There are national providers, such as Netcom, AT&T, and Earthlink, which give you the basic Internet services through their own software, and unlimited time online for about twenty dollars per month. There are also regional and local providers. Almost all of them will provide you with a software package to log on to the Internet. The cost will be about the same as for a national provider. Most of the ISPs will also charge a one-time setup fee, usually about twenty-five dollars.

For the rest of this lesson we're going to concentrate on the ISP access. Whether you decide to use a commercial online service, or a national service as your provider, the Internet functions will be almost the same.

CYBERSARGE SAYS:

Right about now would be a perfect time to take this book to your parents or your teacher and have them read **Chapter 9: Where Are Your Kids Tonight on the Net? (page 183),** *which is a grown-ups' guide to their children's involvement in cyberspace.*

CyberSarge steps back into the center of the computer screen. "Once you've selected your service provider, the technical support staff will give you the information you need to connect to the Internet. However, most packages for getting online have on-screen instructions that are easy to follow without outside help."

Kate and Zack tell CyberSarge that they need to do some research about online services. (Refer to *Chapter 6: Getting Outfitted, page 95.*) Then they need to talk to their parents since most online accounts need to be held by an adult. Providers often require a credit card number so they can automatically charge your monthly fee and your time online. Children can get their own e-mail addresses under the adult's account, but adults need to be included in this process.

CYBERSARGE SAYS:

There is a lot of information, like the exact Internet address of your ISP, that your computer needs to know. Fortunately, most ISPs will give you a program that enters all the information for you. If you need to do this yourself, a list of the steps will come from your Internet service provider with the start-up packet.

Once Kate and Zack figure out which online service and account would work best for their needs, they talk to their parents about how much time they will be allowed online every week. (If you are trying to get your school hooked up to the Internet, you would have this conversation with your teacher or principal.) Their parents may have different ideas about which service is the best for the whole family, especially if they choose to use the Internet as well.

The family sits down and discusses all the options and reaches an agreement about the time the kids are allotted every week. Since time online means that the telephone line will be tied up (unless you have a phone line dedicated to the computer) Kate and Zack's parents give them a specific schedule of hours they can go online during the day.

Their parents also set limits for the kids about appropriate places for them to visit online; Kate and Zack agree not to visit Internet sites that have adult content, which is not acceptable for children.

Next, Kate and Zack's parents telephone the agreed-upon service provider to set up an account. The service provider promises to send out the necessary software and a start-up manual to their home within a few days. However, Zack and Kate could have gone to their local software store and bought commercial programs that would provide the same start-up material.

When all the information arrives, their parents hand them the package, and Kate and Zack rush over to their computer. Now they are ready to continue with their lesson!

"Okay," says Kate. "We've selected a service provider in our city called MyNet. What do we do now?"

CyberSarge speaks to them from the screen. "Install your software and get it running," he says. "I'll be here to help you if you need me."

Kate puts the disk in the drive and types: A:SETUP (or A:INSTALL).

In response, the set-up program copies several programs to their computer's **hard drive**. The first is the **TCP/IP** program, which allows their computer to connect with their Internet service provider.

Kate and Zack watch as the setup program enters in their e-mail and newsgroup addresses. Since this is a new account, this part is very easy.

One thing the program won't do is give Kate and Zack their **user names** and passwords. Kate has selected *kate* as her user name. Sometimes the name you want to use will already have been taken by

HARD DRIVE

This is a disk drive that reads and writes from hard disks.

TCP/IP

Transmission Control Protocol/Internet Protocol is the language that allows communication between all the different computers on the Internet. TCP/IP is actually a set of instructions that tells each computer how to send and receive packets of information, which often have to travel through multiple networks in order to reach their destinations. TCP/IP also checks that the information gets delivered in one piece, without errors. It's not necessary to know how TCP/IP works, only that you need to have it.

CYBERSARGE SAYS:

At this point, rather than listing step-by-step instructions here that you might have to follow, which will vary depending upon which ISP you select, we've moved the technical details to Chapter 8: Tech Talk (page 161). *In* Tech Talk *you will find specific steps on how to set up your Internet service.*

someone else. If there had been another Kate using this server, our Kate might have selected **kate1** as her user name. You can use practically whatever name you want. Be creative! Just remember that this is what identifies you when you're online. Kate chooses a password also. We won't tell you what her password is, and when she types it in, it looks like ***** on the screen, so no one looking over her shoulder can read it.

"All right!" Zack exclaims when the setup program finishes. "Let's blast off!"

Zack and Kate both grab for the mouse. Kate wins. She clicks on the word *Connect* and their **modem** dials the number of their service provider. They both watch anxiously for a moment—then the computer beeps as it makes contact.

"Congratulations, Cadets," CyberSarge tells them proudly. "You're on the Internet! But before you do any real surfing on the Net, you'll need to know more about Internet addresses. We'll cover that in the next section."

USER NAME

User name is the name you use to log on to a network. Usually your ISP or commercial service has given you permission to log on to the network and has recorded your user name in the network's databank. That way other users can check to find out when you are actively using the network.

MODEM

Modem stands for modulator-demodulator. It's a device that allows your computer to link up with other computers over telephone lines.

Chapter 3

Pilot's Manual for the Internet:

Getting Connected

Finally the big day arrives. Today Kate and Zack are going to take their first cruise on the Internet. They have selected a local service provider, MyNet, as their Internet gateway. Each of them has his or her own personal address on the Internet. Kate's is ***kate@mynet.com***, and Zack's is ***zack@mynet.com***.

They have learned that every personal Internet address has three parts:

1. The user name (like ***kate*** or ***zack***, or even something strange like ***UU2020***).

2. The @ sign, which means "at."

3. The address of the user's mail server, which is usually the server's **domain name**.

Kate's user name is ***kate*** and on the Internet she is known as "kate at mynet dot com," which looks like:

kate@mynet.com

The ***mynet.com*** part of the address is called the domain name. The domain name is based on the Internet Protocol, or IP system.

CYBERSARGE SAYS:

When telling someone your e-mail address, say the word "at" for the @, and say "dot" instead of "period." Kate's e-mail address (kate@mynet.com) is spoken as: "Kate at mynet dot com."

IP addresses have been established so that every server on the Internet has its own unique address. Some user names can be as long as ten characters. If Kate and Zack shared an address, it could be:

kateandzac@mynet.com

Addresses are read from left to right. Everything to the right of the @ sign is called the domain. The word on the left of the @ sign is the user name. Sometimes domain names can be very long—like *one.two.univ.edu*—but each letter and number to the right of the @ is all part of the domain name.

All IP addresses have four sets of numbers separated by periods, like: 999.200.8.100. These numbers mean the same thing as something like **mynet.com**—but whereas people find it easier to remember a name they can say and spell, computers are more comfortable with numbers.

Well, it's pretty easy to figure out what the **mynet** part of the domain name is. But what about the **com** part? The **com** part of the address tells you that **mynet** is a commercial site. Here is a list of domain abbreviations:

- *edu* for educational sites, like colleges
- *com* for commercial sites, like companies
- *gov* for government sites, like the White House or the Library of Congress
- *mil* for military sites, like the Pentagon
- *net* for network administrative sites, which are networks running other networks
- *org* for organizational sites, like public and non-profit groups
- *firm* for businesses or firms
- *store* for online stores
- *web* for groups dealing with WWW-related activities.

DOMAIN NAME

The official Internet name used by organizations and individuals as the cyberspace location for their Web sites. Many domain names end in **.com** (pronounced "dot com"), **.org**, or **.edu**.

arts for groups involved in cultural and
entertainment activities

rec for groups involved in recreational and
sports activities

info for groups providing information services

nom for those who want individual or personal
names

Sometimes you will see an address that ends in
something like *edu.uk*. The *uk* means that the
address is in England, also known as the United
Kingdom; *au* means Australia, and *fr* means France.
A domain without a two-letter code usually means
that the site is in the United States. Some country
codes you may encounter include:

aq Antarctica

ar Argentina

br Brazil

cn China

et Ethiopia

hk Hong Kong

il Israel

it Italy

in India

jp Japan

ke Kenya

mx Mexico

nz New Zealand

es Spain

th Thailand

uk United Kingdom

us United States (hardly ever used)

va Vatican City

Sometimes you may see an address that looks like
mach1.mynet.com. The *mach1* means that it is a
subdomain, which means it belongs to another

CYBERSARGE SAYS:

While your dial-up program, the program in your Internet software that connects to the Internet, may let you "save" your secret password so you don't have to type it in each time, it's better to type it in every time you log on. After all, it's not a secret if anyone can read it and use it.

computer that is located within the mynet local network of computers. In our example, ***mach1*** is part of mynet.

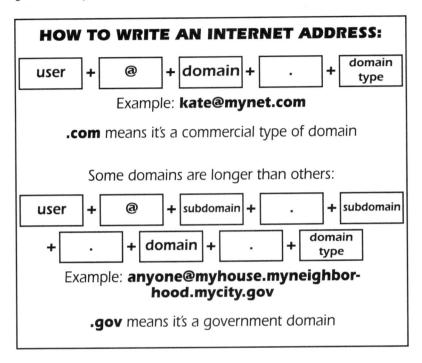

HOW TO WRITE AN INTERNET ADDRESS:

| user | + | @ | + | domain | + | . | + | domain type |

Example: **kate@mynet.com**

.com means it's a commercial type of domain

Some domains are longer than others:

| user | + | @ | + | subdomain | + | . | + | subdomain |
| + | . | + | domain | + | . | + | domain type |

Example: **anyone@myhouse.myneighbor-hood.mycity.gov**

.gov means it's a government domain

"That's not so difficult," Zack says confidently.

CyberSarge is waiting for the kids down in a corner of the screen. "Let's see how much you've learned. I'll be watching you from down here. If you need me, call me, but otherwise you're on your own for this trip."

Today they will use Kate's account to log on to MyNet. Their gateway software—the dialer program supplied by MyNet—is simple. Kate double clicks on the program icon to start it and when the window opens, she types in her user name and her secret password. Then Kate moves her mouse pointer and clicks on the *Connect* icon. [Note: your icon may vary.]

Yesterday Kate and Zack set up the proper phone numbers and Internet address, so now they just wait while their modem dials. After a moment they hear the continuous static sound that means they're connected. The two modems, their own and the one at MyNet, figure out how to talk to each other. Then the *Connect* icon changes to a *Disconnect* icon. That means they are online! When they want to leave the Internet, they will click on the *Disconnect* icon.

"What's first?" Zack asks his sister.

"Well. . . like CyberSarge keeps telling us, the best place to start is at the beginning." Kate gives her brother an excited smile. "Let's check to see if we have any e-mail."

Kate selects the e-mail item from the menu, and as the program starts, a lesson appears on the screen:

File	Edit		View	

E-MAIL

Almost all e-mail programs do the same things. The problem is almost all of them do it slightly differently. We're not going to be able to discuss all the various command sequences of every e-mail program. Instead we will look at the basic functions most e-mail programs have in common. These basic functions are:

1. Reading the e-mail that is sent to you

2. Saving your e-mail to a file on your computer so you can read it later

3. Printing out your e-mail so you can give a **hard copy** to someone

HARD COPY

Hard copy refers to printing out a paper copy of a computer document on a printer.

FILTERS

Filters are used by software programs to send information to a particular place so you don't have to do it by hand. It operates almost like a coin sorter: You feed nickels, dimes, pennies, and quarters into one part, and the sorter separates the coins into different slots. For example, a filter will take all mail from a particular sender and put it into one special file.

4. Replying to your e-mail letters

5. Writing a brand new e-mail letter to send

6. Attaching files, pictures, or other objects to the e-mail letters you are sending

7. Sending your completed e-mail messages on the Internet

8. Keeping an Internet address book to make it easier to send e-mail messages to people you write to a lot

That's really all any e-mail program does. Some programs make it easier to do these things than others. Some have built-in spell checkers, while others don't. Some, like the commercial version of Eudora, allow you to set up **filters** so mail from a particular mailing list or an Internet key pal will automatically be routed into a special mailbox. For example, you could instruct your e-mail program to send every letter from Julie to a special mailbox that you've named *Julie*. Or you could send all letters that have the phrase "kid news" to a *kid news* mailbox.

Some of the newer e-mail programs let you include graphics and sounds within your e-mail messages. But remember that the person receiving these e-mail messages has to have the same type of software in order to be able to see and hear them.

Before you can read or send e-mail, you need to set up your e-mail program so that it can "talk" to your Internet gateway provider. The first step is for you to click on the *Configuration* menu item. We'll use Eudora as an example, since it works like most e-mail programs. Some programs may call this step *Options, Setup,* or *Preferences.*

THIS WAY

THAT WAY

E-MAIL

Usually you will be asked to enter four kinds of information. We'll go into more detail later on, but we'll go through the basic steps here:

1. **YOUR POP (OR MAIL) ACCOUNT NAME**. This is your Internet address. All of your e-mail gets delivered here. For Kate this is *kate@mynet.com*

2. **YOUR REAL NAME**. Some Internet addresses can be confusing, like: *U913@anynet.com* Even with Kate's address, we don't know which Kate she is. There are thousands of Kates on the Internet. Putting in your real name will tell the people receiving your e-mail exactly who you are. However, to protect your privacy, we suggest using the initial of your last name instead of your entire last name, or your first and middle names with the initial of your last name. **Never enter your full name.**

3. **YOUR SMTP (OR MAIL SERVER)**. This is essentially your local Internet postmaster's address. It is usually something like: *smtp@mynet.com*. When you sign up with a service provider, they will give you this information.

4. **YOUR RETURN ADDRESS**. Usually this is the same as your POP address.

If you can't figure out how to set up your e-mail, call your service provider. They will help you by taking you through all the steps. You should also keep a list, with the information about your Internet gateway server, close to your computer so that you can refer to it whenever the need arises.

Now that you're set up, you should send a message to see if everything is working. The easiest way to check is to send an e-mail to yourself.

POP

POP stands for Post Office Protocol. Internet mail servers act like just like a real post office. They look at the mail that arrives and route it toward its final destination.

SMTP

SMTP stands for Simple Mail Transfer Protocol. SMTP is the language Internet mail servers (or postmasters) use to talk to one another and exchange e-mail letters.

CYBERSARGE SAYS:

Even if you have sub-scribed to a service that charges a flat rate for unlimited time online, it's not a good idea to tie up the phone system for hours. As more and more folks are going online, the traffic on the Internet is becoming like the freeways at rush hour—sometimes everything slows to a crawl. The busiest time on the Internet is usually around 5:00 p.m.

Kate's message to herself would look like this:

> *To: kate@mynet.com*
>
> *From: kate@mynet.com*
>
> *Subject: Test*
>
> *This message is a test.*
>
> *>>Kate*

Okay. Now let's send it.

There will be a menu command or an icon for sending mail. Click on it, and your message is sent.

If you're writing a bunch of messages, most mail programs will allow you to save these in a waiting area so you can e-mail them all at once.

Now that you've sent your e-mail, let's check and see if it's arrived. Since your e-mail is local, and does not have to go out onto the Internet, it's probably already in your e-mailbox.

Click on the file menu item that lets you receive mail. There also may be an icon that pops up saying *You Have New Mail*, or *Read Mail*, or *Get Mail*. Most programs, like Eudora, allow you to download your mail and read it later.

Because the Internet is so large, your local mail server postmaster program has direct connections with only a few other computers on the Net. When an e-mail arrives at one of those directly-connected computers, the postmaster there checks to see if the person you sent the mail to is at that site. If so, the mail is delivered. Otherwise it is routed on to other sites that that computer is directly connected to; it keeps going from computer to computer until it finds the right one. But remember, all of this traveling takes only seconds.

If you look at the top section of the e-mail letters you receive, you can see the routing they took to get your e-mail delivered from there to here.

Since our test letter didn't have to travel anywhere, it was delivered instantly.

Remember that reading your mail and replying to it off-line—when you're not hooked up to your Internet gateway—can save you a lot of online time and some money, too! Also, you won't feel rushed to send off a reply before you've thought about what you want to say.

So now you've got the mail in your mailbox. After you read it, you usually have a few choices:

1. KEEP THE LETTER ON YOUR COMPUTER.

Usually you'll do this by storing it in a *Saved Mail* area. Many e-mail programs allow you to set up several mailboxes where you can store your e-mail letters.

2. REPLY TO THE LETTER. You can do this immediately by clicking on a *Reply* item on the menu, wait until later when you have more time, or write it offline and then log back on to the Internet to send it.

3. TRASH THE LETTER. Just like you do with your paper mail at home (unless, of course, it's recyclable) you can take e-mail letters you're done with and toss them in a trash can . . . only this is an electronic trash can. Some e-mail programs let you retrieve messages from the trash, at least temporarily. It's like throwing something in the waste basket and then getting it out before it gets dumped into the outside trash can and carried away by the garbage collectors.

4. PRINT THE LETTER. You can also select the *Print* item on the menu to print out a hard copy of the e-mail message.

5. SAVE THE LETTER. You can save it to a file and open it later in your word processor.

6. SET UP AN ADDRESS BOOK. Many e-mail programs will let you create an "address book" in

CYBERSARGE SAYS:

A word of warning: Once you "trash" a letter and then exit the e-mail program, it's gone. Forever!

CYBERSARGE SAYS:

You can use nicknames to send multiple e-mail letters to several people at once by assigning several addresses to one nickname. For example, both julie@mynet.com, and sam@mynet.com could be stored under the nickname "School Pals."

which you can enter the Internet addresses of the people you write to most often. It's much simpler to select an address from a list of already-saved addresses than to type in the whole address each time. And if you misspell the address, your e-mail will never be delivered. Most of the time, the mail server will return the e-mail letter to you as undeliverable, just like the real post office, but sometimes the letter will just vanish into cyberspace.

"There's one other function that e-mail lets you do," CyberSarge says. "E-mail lets you subscribe to mailing lists."

"I've heard about mailing lists," says Zack, nodding. "But I don't quite understand them."

"Mailing lists operate in two ways," replies CyberSarge. "The first way is through newsgroup newsletters and it's like subscribing to a magazine. The newsgroup newsletter pops up in your Internet mailbox once a day, or once a month, depending upon how often it gets published. You usually do not participate in writing or putting together the information it provides."

"I know what the second way is," Kate pipes in. "It's when a group of people who like to talk about the same thing start a mailing list discussion group."

"Right. These are similar to newsgroups. The difference is that anyone can read the messages in a newsgroup, but you have to subscribe to a mailing list. All the messages go into a Listserver and then get sent to everyone who has subscribed to the mailing list."

"What's a Listserver?" asks Zack.

"You're one step ahead of me again, Zack," CyberSarge says with a grin.

File	Edit		View	

MAILING LISTS

What is a Listserver mailing list? Quite simply, it is a list of a lot of people who share similar interests and want to receive and/or exchange e-mail messages with the group.

Anyone can subscribe to a list by sending a *Subscribe* command to the Listserv address. Any e-mail letter sent to the list's address is copied and mass-mailed to the e-mail mailbox of every person who subscribes to the list. Everyone else on the list can then reply to that letter.

Listserver mailing lists give you a way to have open discussions with dozens, even hundreds of people who share similar interests.

When using Listservers you have to remember there are two different addresses:

1. The list address is the address you send something to if you want it to be sent to everyone else who subscribes to the list. The address would look like: *baseball@mynet.com* if the subject were baseball.

2. The Listserv address is the address you send all of your commands to and would look like: *listserv@mynet.com*

The more common commands you might send to a Listserv address include:

A. Subscribe to subscribe to the mailing list. This would look like: *subscribe listname <your user name>*

B. Unsubscribe to unsubscribe to a mailing list you have previously subscribed to. This looks like: *unsubscribe listname*

C. Get to a file from the mailing list. This would look like: *get filename filetype*

D. Index will get you a list of the files that are available on the mailing list. This would look like:

index listname

Always remember to:

1. SEND YOUR LETTERS TO THE LIST ADDRESS. This is like a post office sorting machine that distributes mail to everyone on the mailing list. Don't send commands here.

2. SEND YOUR COMMANDS TO THE LISTSERV ADDRESS. This is like a postmaster who sends you the document you asked for. Don't send letters here.

"But how do we find out what mailing lists are on the Internet?" asks Kate.

"That's not always so easy," replies CyberSarge. "There are so many of them. One of the best sources is to subscribe to a newsgroup that talks about mailing lists. Usually they will have an FAQ file you can download to your computer."

"What's an FAQ?" Zack asks CyberSarge.

"FAQ stands for Frequently Asked Questions. A FAQ is usually a text file, often with the filename suffix *.faq* that has questions and answers about a particular topic. You can sometimes find them in Usenet newsgroups. And that's part of your next lesson," CyberSarge says and smiles.

File	Edit		View

USENET NEWSGROUPS AND NEWSREADERS

E-mail is usually one-to-one, which means you're sending a personal note to a friend on the Internet. Usenet newsgroups are one-to-many, which means you're posting a message for a lot of people to read.

A newsgroup is a collection of messages with a related theme. You might think of newsgroups like the bulletin boards at school, where you post a message for a lot of people to read.

These newsgroups have become international meeting places on the Internet. They're where people gather to meet their friends, discuss the day's events, keep up with computer trends, or just talk about whatever's on their minds. There are more than 20,000 newsgroups, in several different languages, which discuss everything from art to zoology, from science fiction to knitting.

Some of the main areas of Usenet newsgroups include:

FAQ

FAQs are Frequently Asked Questions. They're the best place to start when you're curious about a subject.

biz	for business
comp	for computers and related subjects
misc	for subjects that don't fit anywhere else
sci	for science
news	for news
rec	for hobbies, games, and recreation
soc	for social and cultural issues
talk	for talking about politics or other topics
alt	for an alternative view
clari	for commercial wire-service stories
k12	for educational information for kindergarten through 12th grade

In addition, many servers carry special newsgroups for their particular cities, states, or regions. For example, in the ***pnw.general*** newsgroup, people who live in the

Pacific Northwest can find news and information related to that part of the country. Within the Pacific Northwest, Seattle, Portland, and Vancouver have their own city newsgroups. In fact, most of the major cities in the United States have at least one newsgroup.

With all these newsgroups, you're bound to find something that is interesting to you. And to help you get started, we've included instructions for finding exciting and interesting newsgroups in *Chapter 7: Guide to the Galaxy (page 121).*

Some newsgroups also contain pictures that you can download as messages and then convert into graphics format. The computer translates the picture into digits (the process is called digitizing) and then untranslates it in your newsreader. Most newsreader groups will translate such files automatically, but if they don't, you can download utility programs that will do it.

When you've decided you want to subscribe to a newsgroup through your service provider, just do the following:

SUBSCRIBING TO A NEWSGROUP

First, you need to get a list of the available newsgroups. You'll find specific instructions for getting newsgroup lists in the *Tech Talk* chapter *(page 161).* Not all servers carry all Usenet newsgroups, but most will carry the basic newsgroups.

Then, to read the messages, you need a newsreader software program. Both Netscape Navigator and Microsoft Internet Explorer have a newsreader as part of their browsers. It is likely that a newsreader program will be included in the software package you purchased, or you can use a stand-alone newsreader such as FreeAgent. You can buy FreeAgent or download it off the Web at: ***http://www.fortinc.com/forte.***

Though they will vary in some ways, every newsreader program will have five basic functions:

1. GET AND UPDATE A LIST OF YOUR AVAILABLE NEWSGROUPS. The first time you select this option on your newsreader program, it's probably going to take a while. Downloading a list of up to 20,000 items can be slow. But you should only have to do it once. From then on you can update the list by asking for only the new groups that have been added since the last time you checked. (Remember to note the date you downloaded the list the first time so that you can refer back to that date when you want to update your list.)

2. SUBSCRIBE AND UNSUBSCRIBE TO NEWSGROUPS. You can either scroll through the downloaded list of available newsgroups and tag those you want to read, or, for quicker results, you can just type in the name manually.

3. READ THE NEWSGROUPS YOU'VE SUBSCRIBED TO. Depending upon your particular newsreader, you can do this online by scrolling through the list of headers (a header is usually the subject of an article) and then clicking on the selected ones to read them, or else you can mark the headers while you're offline and then go back online and download only those articles you've selected.

4. REPLY TO AN ARTICLE OR POST A NEW ONE. This is like using a mailing list. You're sending a message to a group of people who subscribe to this newsgroup. It's like posting a note on your school bulletin board.

5. SAVE SELECTED ARTICLES TO A FILE. When you find something you want to keep, like an FAQ article on a subject that interests you, save it as a file. Later you can use your newsreader or a word-processing program to read it again, or to print out a copy.

Some newsreaders will let you read only selected threads that you've requested.(Remember? A thread is a series of articles on the same subject.)

"Are there any rules for posting articles to a newsgroup?" asks Kate.

"Only the Seven Simple Rules," replies CyberSarge, smiling, "and all of these involve common sense and common courtesy."

File	Edit		View

SEVEN SIMPLE RULES FOR NEWSGROUP POSTING

1. POST IT IN THE RIGHT PLACE. Don't post your thoughts on dog training in the Chinese cooking group.

2. DON'T SPAM. Spamming is sending the same article to everyone **everywhere** on the Internet. You may want to post the same article to one or two groups that are similar—like the Seattle and Pacific Northwest newsgroups—but please don't clutter the Internet with junk mail.

3. KEEP YOUR HEADER SIMPLE AND DIRECT. Don't try to be too cute, just say what your article is about in as few words as possible. You want the people who are interested in what you're talking about to notice, understand, and read your article.

4. SAY WHAT YOU HAVE TO SAY AND THEN STOP. You are busy and so is everyone else on the Internet. You don't have time to read dozens of pages. Make sure you say what you want to say clearly and in the shortest way possible. Then stop!

SPAM

SPAM stands for Sending Particularly Annoying Messages. SPAM is most often advertising. If you ever receive a message advertising a "fantastic business opportunity" from someone you've never heard of, this is SPAM.

5. REFERENCE YOUR MESSAGE TO AN EXISTING

THREAD. Include a sentence or two from a previous article so the other readers will know what you're talking about. On the other hand, you don't want to repeat everything that was previously said on the subject. Referencing is done so that people coming into the middle of the discussion know what you're talking about.

6. TRY NOT TO

SHOUT. TYPING EVERYTHING IN CAPITAL LETTERS IS CONSIDERED SHOUTING. Don't do it. Use capitals only when you want to emphasize a point. If you type everything in capitals, otherwise known as caps, no one will want to read what you have to say.

7. TREAT PEOPLE THE SAME WAY YOU WANT TO BE

TREATED. There will be arguments, and you'll disagree with someone's point-of-view. You'll even get mad. But once you've posted an angry article, you can't unpost it. Your words will be there for everyone to read, and for a long time. So count to ten before making a reply.

"Okay," Kate says, "we can send mail and read articles. What if I just want to talk to someone—like I do on the phone—without having to send a letter, even an electronic one. Can I do that?

"Well," replies CyberSarge. "**UNIX** systems have

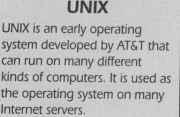

UNIX

UNIX is an early operating system developed by AT&T that can run on many different kinds of computers. It is used as the operating system on many Internet servers.

CYBERSARGE SAYS:

If you like to move around the Internet and meet new people, then IRC is the way to go. You can plug into conversations with kids from all over the world.

something called "talk" that lets different people chat with each other when they both log on. The Internet takes that one step further. Two or more people can get together on an IRC."

File	Edit	View

CHAT

Chat, also known as Internet Relay Chat (IRC), allows you to "talk" in real time with people all over the world.

In computer jargon, "to chat" means to talk online, just like you would having a telephone conversation, only you're typing on your keyboard instead of talking, and your computer screen is doing the listening.

IRC became really popular during the Persian Gulf War. People used IRC to catch up on news updates from around the world that came across the wire. News updates were broadcast on a single channel and people would gather on that channel to read the news reports.

People like IRCs because they let you chat worldwide from any site that is connected to the Internet. Any computer user can connect to an IRC server and communicate with anybody anywhere in the world—right now! Imagine having an online club made up of kids from Russia, Mexico, and Australia!

As recently as a year ago, you had to go through a lot of steps to log on to a chat server. Nowadays, you can log on to a server right through your browser. It's that easy!

One of the main attractions of IRC is that you can create and control your own chats. You can have private online chats with a group of friends, almost like getting together at someone's house—only this house is on the Internet and your guests may be from all over the world!

If you aren't using an Internet program that supports IRC—or chat, as it's generally referred to now—you can get both Windows and Mac shareware programs from several FTP sites on the Internet.

After you install a Chat program, following the instructions that come with the program, you can now choose your chat name. This is the name (not your full real name) by which you'll be known on the chat channels. Then you log on to the Internet as you normally do and log on to a chat server. There is a list of chat programs listed in *Chapter 6: Getting Outfitted (page 95)*.

Once you have logged on, your server may give you some rules or warnings, such as "**Flaming** will NOT be tolerated." Much of what you see may look like gibberish, and a lot of things might be hard to understand at first. Different conversations take place at once; people talk to each other and comment on other people's conversations. It's fast and thrilling to participate in a chat because you never know who's going to say what next! Don't worry, though. The secret is to listen in for a while. This is called **lurking**, which is basically hanging around and seeing what's going on. Then just introduce yourself, using your nickname, such as "Hi everybody, I'm Rockstar1" or "Scrappy555" or whatever name you've chosen. Someone will usually say hello. Another thing you can do is talk to people you DO know. With chat you can set up your own channel and arrange with other members of your family or your friends to join you online at a certain time. If you don't want interruptions during your chats, you can set the channel mode to *Private* to keep strangers from entering your discussions.

CYBERSARGE SAYS:

When you want to chat with someone, remember what time it is in the parts of the world where you're calling. While it may be noon where you are, it could be midnight in your friend's city. Try to schedule a reasonable time for everyone when setting up a chat.

FLAMING

Flaming is using words to stomp on someone in cyberspace for saying something you consider wrong or just plain stupid. It's kind of like slamming the door when you're mad. It's not very nice, either. Don't do it.

LURKING

Lurking is hanging around in the background and watching online discussions without getting involved. Most of us are lurkers when we first enter a new site on the Internet.

"Wow!" Zack looks at Kate. "We gotta try this IRC thing. It's pretty cool to think that we can chat with lots of different people at the same time!"

"Yes, chats are fun, " agrees CyberSarge. "So far you've logged on to your server, read your e-mail, and learned about newsgroups and chat. What I'd like to do next is talk about the World Wide Web. As you may or may not know, this is the greatest resource on the Net."

| File | Edit | View |

WORLD WIDE WEB & WEB BROWSERS

As mentioned before, the World Wide Web (also known as the WWW or just the Web) is the newest and fastest-growing part of the Internet. When you hear people talking about the Internet, what they often mean is the Web. The Web can contain your text, pictures, sound, and even video information.

Think of the Web as a place where anyone can publish electronic magazine pages. Then any computer on the Internet equipped with a Web browser can view these pages. It's the newest and largest form of electronic publishing on the Internet today!

Now imagine that instead of flipping from one page in a magazine to another, you can go from one article in a geography magazine to another in a magazine about history—instantly.

For example, say you're reading about baseball in one document, and you see that the word *Seattle* is underlined or highlighted. Simply click on that key word with your mouse, and you will be taken automatically to a new document that talks about the Seattle Mariners baseball team. And this new document might have other key words that would take you to still more documents, which might be located anywhere in the world.

For instance, Ken Griffey, Jr. plays for Seattle, so you might see his name highlighted, which indicates that his name is a key word. You could then click on his name and jump to a document that talks about him. All this with just a touch of your keyboard or the click of your mouse!

Magic? No. It's all based on something called hypertext, which we discussed earlier. Using hypertext you click on a highlighted word with a mouse and you are taken into an entirely new document.

Using hypertext links, it's possible for you to go surfing around the Web, bouncing from document to document, by clicking your mouse pointer on the key word links in the documents. Jules Verne wrote about going around the world in 80 days. You can accomplish the same feat in minutes!

What is really so special about the Web is that you don't have to know the exact address of where you are, or even how you got there.

The Web is able to accomplish all of this by using something called URLs—Universal Resource Locators. An URL is an address for any Internet resource.

The more common types of URLs that you will encounter are:

http://   for an address on the World Wide Web

gopher://   for an address in Gopherspace

ftp://   for a file directory address

telnet://   for a direct Telnet connection

URLs were created as a universal system for accessing information on the Internet, whether it's a single file on an FTP site, an entire Gopher server, or an image on the Web. That means that while browsing the Web, you're

TELNET

The network terminal protocol that allows you to log on to any other computer on the network anywhere in the world. At Telnet sites, you can only access the information that the site allows you to, unless you already have an account; often university networks work this way, allowing you to access their library information.

BOOKMARKS

You put a bookmark in a page of a book or a magazine so you can get back there easily. It's the same idea on the Net. Using bookmarks in your Web browsers lets you get back to a really interesting page in a single jump. We'll talk more about bookmarks in *Chapter 8: Tech Talk (page 161).*

going to have to get used to seeing and typing things such as:

http://www.library.edu/books/pages.html

The ***http*** means you're dealing with a Web resource. It stands for HyperText Transport Protocol. HTTP is the particular way the Web moves information around the world.

Next comes the name of the site at which the resource is located; here that is ***www.library***, which indicates the World Wide Web library.

Then you find directories and subdirectories listed in the address. In this address, that is ***edu/books/pages***. For instance, ***pages*** is a subdirectory of ***books,*** which is a subdirectory of ***edu***. ***edu*** is the overall education directory at the WWW library. By the way, URLs are often case sensitive, so be careful when typing them. ***Library***, with a capital "L," is not the same as ***library*** with a small "l." Also, when you type an address, remember that it should be typed on one continuous line, with no spaces. There are never any spaces in Internet addresses.

In the above example, notice how the last item ends in ***.html***. That stands for HyperText Markup Language, which is the programming language used to create hypertext links on the Web.

You'll find a lot of Web addresses ending in ***.html***. Sometimes, if you are trying to reach a service without a main HTML page (a gopher server, for example), you may have to end the address with a slash, which looks like this: **/**
That kind of address might look like this:

gopher://gopher.myplace.org/

Luckily, if you **bookmark** an address, you will have to type in these long names only the first time you go to a new address. Once you add a particular address to your bookmark list, then you can instantly jump to it by just clicking on the name in your list.

WEB BROWSERS

To access the Web you'll use a program called a Web browser. Browsers are software tools that let you navigate through the World Wide Web and see graphics and text on your computer screen.

Web browsers can read documents and can also download them to your computer's hard drive. Later in the book, you'll find out how these browsers can access files using FTP, read Usenet newsgroups, and Telnet into remote computer sites. In short, Web browsers let you travel through cyberspace and do almost everything you want.

While there are a lot of Web browsers that you can use, Netscape Navigator and Microsoft's Internet Explorer are the most popular.

A. NETSCAPE NAVIGATOR

Netscape Navigator is one of the best Web browsers around—and for good reason. It is loaded with features, and has its own e-mail, newsgroup, and built-in FTP programs. It also has **plug-in** programs, like chat. You can find a list of detailed plug-ins in *Chapter 6: Getting Outfitted (page 95).*

B. MICROSOFT INTERNET EXPLORER

Microsoft came to the Internet late, but since it arrived it has become better (and more and more people are using it) with every new version. Internet Explorer also comes loaded with the same features as Netscape Navigator.

If you use the latest version of either one of these browsers you won't be unhappy. It's likely that your Internet service provider will supply you with one of these programs when you sign up to go online.

DID YOU KNOW THAT?

It is predicted that by the beginning of the new millennium (the year 2000) the number of Internet users will be more than 160 million.

PLUG-INS

An add-on program for Web browsers to increase their usefulness. Some plug-ins allow sound to be played when you link to a Web page. Other plug-ins run video images. However, your computer must have the capable hardware, such as enough memory and a fast modem, to use some of these plug-ins.

"I can't wait to browse the Web," announces Zack as the lesson ends. Kate's broad smile is a clear sign that she's as excited as her little brother.

"Web browsers, even those as sophisticated as Netscape Navigator or Microsoft Internet Explorer, can't do everything by themselves," CyberSarge explains. "So that's where plug-ins come in."

"What's a plug-in?" Zack asks.

"Plug-ins got started with version 2.0 of Netscape Navigator. They are extensions to your regular browser program."

"Like a spell checker is to a word processor?" Kate wonders.

"Right," CyberSarge says. "Plug-ins are programs that attach themselves to your Web browser and do special things. For example, RealAudio's Player plug-in starts up whenever the browser encounters a special Real Audio formatted file. And then it plays those files right over your computer speaker."

"Just like listening to the radio online," Zack says.

"Exactly!" says CyberSarge. "Here's more about plug-ins."

File	Edit		View	

PLUG-IN AND PLAY

Plug-ins come in several types. We'll take a quick look at some of the more popular varieties here, and later on, in *Chapter 6: Getting Outfitted (page 95)*, we'll list the most useful ones and where to get them.

A. MULTIMEDIA: The Web Is Alive

The Web is not just words and pictures anymore. It's becoming a multimedia machine with the coming of programs like Java and Shockwave. Multimedia means that text, pictures, sounds, and even movies can all be viewed and listened to on your computer. For example, you can play mini-movies online or download them to view later, using plug-ins like Apple's QuickTime.

B. JAVA (No, it's not coffee!)

Everyone's talking about Java. But what is it?

Well, in simple terms, Java is a programming language that was developed by Sun Microsystems and introduced in January, 1996. What Java does is let you hear sounds and see moving images on your Web browser. Both Netscape and Microsoft support Java in their newest browsers.

When you go on to a **Java-enhanced site**, which is one that supports Java, a Java applet (a kind of mini-program) is downloaded on to your computer. Then whenever you click on to a Java icon, you can see an animated image or video clip, perhaps even with stereo sound in the background. In the age of the Internet, Java is still new, and its full impact is yet to be seen. Also, to run Java applets you're going to have to have a fast computer and a lot of memory.

JAVA-ENHANCED SITE

A Java-enhanced site has Java programs to run animation. It's important to remember that to run Java programs effectively, your computer must have minimum 16 megabytes of RAM (memory). Also, your Web browser should be at least a 3.0 version.

STREAMING AUDIO

In the early days of the Internet, you had to wait for an entire sound file to download before you could hear it. Streaming audio lets you hear the digitized sound as it's broadcast over the Net.

C. ACTIVE-X

Active-X is Microsoft's own Java system, and it's bundled inside their newest Internet Explorer Web browser. Some Web sites, like the official Star Trek site on the Microsoft Network, are using Active-X. You'll need Internet Explorer to view it properly.

D. SOUND: Hear It Now!

Not only can you see things on the Web, now you can hear them, too! You can listen to your favorite sports team play live, or even listen to a radio station online. This is called **streaming audio**, and you'll need a software plug-in, like RealAudio, to do this. You can often download audio files and replay them later on your computer. Of course, you'll still need an audio software program.

E. REALAUDIO

Once upon a time you could read words and see pictures on the Internet. Now, thanks to RealAudio and similar plug-ins, you can hear the Web as well. There's news, music, old radio serials—everything that you ever wanted (or didn't want) to hear. Warner Brothers, for example, replays the old Superman radio shows on their Web site, with a new episode every other week. There are also radio stations broadcasting live on the Web from every corner of the globe. In *Chapter 6: Getting Outfitted (page 95)*, CyberSarge has included a list of some of the plug-ins and helper applications he thinks are the most helpful—and fun.

"Just think, I can listen to a radio station broadcasting from Canada!" exclaims Zack.

"You sure can," says CyberSarge as he reappears on the computer screen, "and you can download RealAudio files. They end in *.ra*, and you can listen to them offline, or even in the background while you're using another program."

"This stuff sounds like a lot of fun," says Kate, "but how can I use the Internet when I need help with my homework? Is the Web the only way for me to get help?"

"I thought you'd never ask," CyberSarge smiles. "One of the best ways to search for information on almost any subject is through Gopherspace."

File	Edit		View	

GOPHERS (DIGGING IT UP IN GOPHERSPACE)

Gopher is a menu-driven program that allows you to hop around the world looking for information through the Internet. Like a real Gopher that burrows through the ground seeking out buried treasures, Gopher burrows through cyberspace, which, in the case of Gophers, is often called Gopherspace.

Gopher programs are designed to search through Gopher servers around the world for the information you're looking for. You can jump from one Gopher server to another by simply clicking on items on the Gopher menu. When you find a document that interests you, you can read it online or download it to your computer to read later.

Gopher servers contain all kinds of interesting and helpful information. For example, some libraries and bookstores maintain Gopher servers with information about the books they carry. Other Gopher servers have been set up to carry documents on a particular subject, such as medicine or

CYBERSARGE SAYS:

Because Gophers are very popular, using a Gopher can often be slow because so many people are trying to use the same Gopher server at the same time. One trick to remember is that your search will go faster if you pick a Gopher server somewhere in the world where it's nighttime. For instance, if you're in the United States and it's afternoon, look for a Gopher server in England or Italy. Remember, on the Internet, calling overseas is just a local call.

DIRECTORIES

The hard drive on your computer is divided into directories. Each directory can contain many different files. If you think of your computer's hard drive like a file cabinet, then directories are drawers in that cabinet.

baseball. When you start up the Gopher program on your computer, it will display a list, often called a *Gopher menu*, of Gopher servers that are available to be searched. You then pick the Gopher server that you want to go to. For instance, if you go to the University of Washington's Gopher server you would see a list of the documents available to you on the University's Gopher server.

"I think I'm going to like Gophering!" exclaims Kate, who already has a list of things she wants to look up. "It's a great way to find out things for my homework assignments."

"And it seems really easy to use," adds Zack.

"It is," CyberSarge assures them. "The people who designed the Gopher system knew that some of the students and teachers who would be searching through Gopherspace were going to be computer newbies, so they wanted to make the program simple."

"Gophers seem great for getting documents, but what if I want to find a game program and download it?" asks Zack.

"Then you need FTP," CyberSarge says and points to their next lesson on the screen.

File	Edit	View

FTP

FTP stands for File Transfer Protocol and allows you to access remote computers and retrieve files from these computers.

What sort of files are available through FTP? Well, there are hundreds of systems connected to the Internet that have file libraries, or archives, accessible to the public. Many of the files in these archives consist of free or low-cost programs for almost every kind of computer. If you want a new software program for your IBM or Macintosh, or if you feel like playing a new game, you'll probably be able to get it using FTP.

There are huge libraries of online documents as well. Copies of historical documents, from the Magna Carta to the Declaration of Independence, are also yours for the downloading. You can also find song lyrics, poems, and even summaries of every episode ever made of your favorite animated TV series.

Your Web browser will let you find and download an FTP file, so you probably won't need a special program. But there are some stand-alone FTP programs available for downloading, and they may be more convenient if you're going to do a lot of file transferring.

The basic steps of any FTP session are:

1. **START UP YOUR FTP PROGRAM** by double-clicking on its icon.

2. **GIVE YOUR FTP PROGRAM THE ADDRESS** you want to connect to.

3. **IDENTIFY YOURSELF** with your user name when you connect to the remote computer. If you don't have an account, try to log on as a guest.

4. **TELL THE REMOTE SITE YOUR PASSWORD** if you have an account there, or try guest again.

5. **USE THE REMOTE COMPUTER'S HELP MENUS** for instructions on how to move through the directories.

6. **CHANGE DIRECTORIES AND LOOK AROUND FOR FILES** you might want to download.

ASCII

ASCII, or American Standard Code for Information Interchange, is a standard computer language, which means that all computers, no matter what type, can "read" it. It allows different computer programs to transfer files. ASCII files are made up of only text.

BINARY

This is a number system that uses only 1's and 0's. It is the system used by computers to communicate information and to transfer files.

CYBERSARGE SAYS:

If you try to get into an FTP directory where you're not supposed to be, you'll either be asked for a password or just not allowed to enter. FTP sites are like hotels; everyone can use the lobby and restaurant, but you have to have a key to get into one of the rooms.

README FILES

Readme files are text files, often found on FTP sites, that explain what is in an FTP directory or that provide other useful information. You also get readme files with computer software, often explaining things you need to know that are not in the printed instruction manual.

7. SET THE TRANSFER MODE WHEN YOU FIND A FILE you want to download. This is usually **ASCII** for plain text files, or **binary** for other types of files, such as programs and pictures.

8. DOWNLOAD THE FILE you want, then continue to search for and download other files.

9. FINALLY, QUIT WHEN YOU'RE ALL DONE.

Chances are you won't have an account with the remote computer site. So how do you log in as a guest or visitor? Well, almost all remote computer sites that allow outside access use the user identification *anonymous*.

By using the name *anonymous*, you are telling that FTP site that you aren't a regular user of that site, but you would still like to access that FTP site, look around, and retrieve files.

So, when your FTP program asks for *User*, you will type in the word: *anonymous*.

Now you need to enter your password. If you log on as *anonymous*, you need to use your full Internet address for your password. Kate would type in:

kate@mynet.com

Many FTP programs will allow you to set up using *anonymous* and your password together, so you only have to do it once. If your FTP program doesn't allow this, you will have to enter both each time once you've made contact with the remote computer.

Once you're logged on to the FTP computer, you will normally find yourself in the main directory. If there is a **readme file**, you can download it on to your computer as an ASCII (or plain text) file and read it on your computer screen without disconnecting from the FTP site. This file usually will tell you something about the files available at this site.

Most public files are located in a directory named **pub**.

To get there you will enter: cd/pub.

You can use the *cd* command, which stands for *change directory*, to travel up and down through the remote computer site's directories until you get to where you want to be. It's kind of like riding an elevator. If you're using your Web browser to visit an FTP site, you can double-click your mouse pointer on the parent directory to move up, or on one of the list of subdirectories to move down.

When you've decided to get a file—in other words to download it to your computer—you should use the binary option. That way you know it will be readable. If you download a program file in ASCII format, you won't be able to use it. A good rule is to always use the binary option, unless you're just going to look at a readme or index file. Your program will tell you how to choose one or the other.

EXTRA STUFF

There are hundreds of plug-ins and helper applications that you can add on to your Web browsers, and more are coming online every day.

Some of these let you check your spelling, offer virus protection when you're downloading software, and let you view files in almost every format invented. Others are fun add ons, like Earthtime, which is a clock that tells you what time it is—in any part of the world. And if you happen to have a camera hooked up to your computer, there are programs that will let you do live video conferencing from home. That way you can see exactly who you're talking with!

Put sight and sound together and you can go online to witness a live concert, be part of a space-shuttle mission, or even take a virtual trip down a raging river in Ethiopia.

Today on the World Wide Web, you can participate in

live, online chats by visiting three-dimensional rooms. HTML (HyperText Markup Language) has evolved into VRML (Virtual Reality Markup Language.) Think of HTML like watching television because it is two-dimensional. But VRML takes this one step further because it is three-dimensional. It's like being *inside* the television.

Virtual reality worlds are becoming some of the hottest sites on the Web. Using avatars, which are like game pieces that you choose to represent you, these multimedia landscapes are open for you to wander through and interact with other avatars. Think of avatars like the playing pieces on a board game. You can't actually visit Boardwalk on your Monopoly board, but your avatar can do it for you. You'll need a fast modem and a powerful computer to properly experience them. But we've put the Web addresses of some of the most popular sites in *Chapter 7: Guide to the Galaxy (page 121)*.

"Okay, Cadets," says CyberSarge, "I think you know enough to try your wings. Now it's time for you two to start navigating the Net and see how much you've learned."

Chapter 4

Navigating the Internet:

Seek and You Shall Find

Kate and Zack are feeling really excited before their first cruise on the Net. But Zack is a little worried.

"The Internet is so big," Zack tells his sister. "Even with everything we've learned, how do you find anything out there in cyberspace? What I'd like to find is some stuff on Egypt for a history report in school."

Zack knows the Web has something about everything somewhere. But where can he find *this* information?

At that moment, CyberSarge pops up on screen. "You need a search engine," he tells him.

"What's a search engine?" Kate asks.

"Let me explain," CyberSarge says as he begins another one of his helpful mini-lessons.

CYBERSARGE SAYS:

Netscape Navigator calls them Bookmarks, but Microsoft Internet Explorer refers to them as Favorites. They're the same thing, though.

File	Edit	View

SEARCH ENGINES (SIMPLE AND ADVANCED)

There are usually three reasons you go searching on the Internet:

1. TO FIND SOMETHING GENERAL. Let's say you have an idea of what you want to look for. For example, you might need some basic information about World War II for a history report. You would look in just the same way you might go window shopping, in which you're not looking for anything in particular.

2. TO FIND SOMETHING SPECIFIC. If you're looking for pictures to download of the Shoemaker-Levy comet that collided with Jupiter, this time you're not just window shopping, you're looking for something specific.

3. TO JUST LOOK AROUND. Say you're just browsing and you want to see what's out there on the Internet. You might go shopping without a shopping list, but you might come across that great present for your Mom!

Search engines are programs on the Internet that help you find what you're looking for. They come in two basic flavors: simple and advanced. Yahoo is a good example of the simple kind because its database is organized by category. If you're looking for information on Kenya you simply enter the word *Kenya*, and Yahoo searches through that already organized category and will retrieve the information from its own files. That's usually enough for most searches.

Other search engines, like Digital's Alta Vista, go out on the Internet and pull up everything that contains the key word you're searching for. This search engine is unlike Yahoo because it does not pull out information from its own files. If you entered the word *Kenya*, any document containing that word, like *Kenyan coffee*, will come up. That's why it is better to be specific when you search.

Some search engines are advanced. You can type in a phrase, like *baby elephants born in zoos*. Rather than find every mention of each of those words, these search engines find only sites that talk about *elephant babies in zoos*. In other words, they try to figure out exactly what you're really looking for.

BOOKMARKS (HOW DO I GET BACK?)

Hansel and Gretel dropped bread crumbs as they wandered through the woods so that they could find their way home again. Unfortunately for them, the birds came along and ate the crumbs.

But there are no birds in your computer. Maybe a few bugs, but let's hope they have small appetites, and won't nibble on the bookmarks you leave so you can return to your favorite place in cyberspace.

Wandering through the Internet is a lot like trudging through an unexplored forest. Bookmarks are a way to mark your path so you can get back to a great place.

Making a bookmark is very simple. When you've arrived at a page you think you'll want to return to, click on the *Bookmarks* or *Favorites* menu, and select the *Add* item.

If you have only a few favorite places, it will be easy to bring up the bookmarks menu and then double-click on the desired link—and off you go.

But it's more likely that you'll soon have a huge and unwieldy file because there are so many interesting places that you'll want to return to. When your bookmark file

CYBERSARGE SAYS:

When you're organizing your bookmarks, you can do it offline. Just start up your Web browser, cancel the dialer routine (that's when your computer calls up your Internet host), and then select the Bookmarks (or Favorites) menu.

CYBERSARGE SAYS:

When you reorganize your bookmarks, you can also rename them. The original name is the one that the Web site puts in its header, but this can sometimes be long and even confusing, like The Los Angeles Old Time Museum of Odds and Ends and Other Stuff. *You can call it whatever makes sense to you, like* simply Old Time Museum. *To do this, go into the bookmarks list on your Web browser and choose the rename function.*

gets too big, you probably will need to organize your Favorites, or Bookmarks, into folders. It's kind of like putting folders into a filing cabinet, with a folder for each of your categories: homework, games, travel, sports, etc.

CACHING

Caching is your Web browser's way of making your Web walks go faster. Whenever you visit a new Web page, the text and pictures from that page are loaded onto your computer and stored in a cache, which is a kind of temporary storage bin on your computer. The next time you visit that page, the Web browser looks in the cache to see if you've been there before. If you have, and if nothing has changed on the page since your last visit, your browser loads the text and pictures from your hard drive, making everything appear on screen a lot quicker.

The problem with caching is that if you do a lot of browsing, the cached files can take up a lot of hard drive space. You should go into your Web browser's options menu and set the amount of hard drive space you want available to use for caching. If your cache gets too big, you can delete the files in it by going into the cache file on your hard drive. This won't create any problems, though the next time you open a Web page it might take a little more time to load.

CACHE
Hardware or software storage in computers that keeps track of the most-recently used data to speed up operations.

Kate leans back in her chair and looks over at her brother. "This is really amazing! There's so much to see and explore."

"The Internet is definitely the coolest," Zack agrees.

"I'd like to try searching Yahoo for some jokes that I could e-mail to my friend Turtle. Can I try?" she asks CyberSarge.

"Of course. After all, the best way to learn the

Internet is to actually dive in and start surfing!" CyberSarge replies.

Kate logs on and waits to be connected. When she's connected, she goes to Yahoo's site at *http://www.yahoo.com* so she can begin her search.

Yahoo's home page comes on the screen and Kate and Zack see different headings at the top labeled *Categories, Sites, AltaVista Web Pages, Headlines,* and *Net Events*. Each heading will take them to more Web pages. For instance, if Kate double-clicked her mouse on *Categories*, a list of subjects such as *Entertainment* or *Sports*, would appear on the screen. Kate could then click on entertainment to find more specific entertainment subjects.

Since Kate is looking for something simple like jokes, she enters the word **jokes** in the blank bar located underneath all the headings. She waits as the computer does its search. What appears on the screen is a phrase that says, *Found 23 Category and 681 Site Matches for jokes*. What this means is that 681 Web sites contain jokes and there are 23 categories for Kate to choose from. Underneath this phrase are all the categories.

Kate scrolls down the categories and picks *Entertainment:Humor, Jokes, and Fun*. She double-clicks and a huge list of jokes appears on the screen:

CYBERSARGE SAYS:

If you go to the same Web pages frequently, then a big hard drive cache can speed things up. But if you're visiting new sites all the time, a smaller hard drive cache is a better idea.

File	Edit	View

Q: What do you call a boomerang that doesn't come back?

A: A stick!

CyberSarge, Kate, and Zack all laugh at this joke and Kate prints out a copy so she can e-mail it to Turtle later.

"If you look at the bottom of this Web page, you'll see that Yahoo lists other search engines, in case you want to search elsewhere," says CyberSarge.

"Yeah, it lists Alta Vista, Lycos, WebCrawler, and lots more," notes Zack.

CyberSarge smiles. "That's the great thing about the Internet—almost anything can be found!"

Part II

Explorer:
Living and Learning in Cyberspace

O:-) <:-) :-) =:-) :-o :-! :-' :-D :-* :-p (:-& :--

CyberSarge looks at Kate and Zack after they return from their tour of the Internet. "You guys did a really good job out there," praises CyberSarge. "Your training phase is nearly over, and now you're ready to pilot your own computer on solo missions through the Internet."

Kate and Zack look at each other excitedly. They're proud of their achievements so far, and can't wait to get out there again. They know that with the help of their pilot's manual and all of the built-in helping devices on the Internet, they will have even more fun the second time.

"Even though you two have come a long way in your training," CyberSarge informs them, "there is still a little more to learn. Read on, Cadets. You're almost there!"

Chapter 5:

The Top Ten Rules for Surfing the Net

Before they can graduate from Cyberspace Academy, Kate and Zack need to learn the ten basic rules for being online. CyberSarge posts a note on the computer for Kate and Zack:

File	Edit	View

CYBERSARGE'S TOP TEN RULES FOR SURFING THE NET

Like driving on the streets of your hometown, cyberspace requires following a few "rules of the road." These are not difficult to learn, and they all have to do with being courteous to other drivers on the Internet.

You've already discovered that the Net is huge and new. It's easy to get lost in it. It's also easy to forget to use our common sense when we're navigating in cyberspace. Since we were little, our parents have told us not to talk to strangers. Well, here we are in a universe of strangers, chatting away. It seems so harmless. But that's not always so. We know from unhappy experiences on the school playground not to pick fights with people. Yet there are people who pick fights on the Internet. They're called *flamers* and picking a fight is called *flaming*.

In general, cyberspace is like an unsupervised playground. And, just like in the offline playground world, there are bullies on the Internet. There are a few nasties lurking in cyberspace who are ready to take advantage of someone if they can.

So how do we deal with them?

Just like home, or school, the Internet has rules to help keep us out of trouble. The rules of cyberspace aren't necessarily written down in a special list. But you'll learn them fast enough as you surf the Net. Most of the rules for using the Internet involve the same common sense and common courtesy you use offline. The cyberspace rules in this book are more like guidelines to help us live together peacefully in cyberspace.

Here's CyberSarge's list of Top Ten Rules for Surfing the Net:

1. NEVER GIVE OUT PERSONAL INFORMATION.

While online, don't tell anyone anything that you wouldn't tell a stranger. It's OK to say "I have brown hair and brown eyes and I'm tall." But it's **not** okay to give out your phone number, your address, or your password. *Even if you know you can trust the person you're chatting with, there may be others who are able to read your e-mail.* This means that even while chatting with a new friend, sending e-mail, or posting messages, **you have to be careful**.

2. AVOID UNPLEASANT SITUATIONS.

Sometimes people feel that because they're talking with people on the computer and not face-to-face, they can be

rude and nasty. It's often tempting to be nasty right back. **Don't!**

You are not required to answer rude or unasked-for messages. Ignoring them is the best way to make them stop. If you get hassled online, tell the operator who runs the computer system or bulletin board about it. Some kinds of mail-reading software have a **twit filter**, which can be activated to eliminate messages from users that you have already had bad experiences with. Use the twit filter whenever necessary.

TWIT FILTER

This is a sorting system in an e-mail program that you use to catch letters from someone you don't want to hear from, or to trash junk e-mail.

3. ALWAYS BE YOURSELF.

You might want to pretend you're somebody else when you're online. It's natural to want to impress others with how cool we are. But trying to fool other people not only prevents others from finding out about us, but also keeps us from seeing others as they really are. Playing fair online means saying, "I'm being real. I hope you are, too."

4. KEEP TRACK OF YOUR TIME.

Being online takes time. You have a life offline as well as in cyberspace. Just make sure you don't overdo it.

Tell yourself to stick to whatever allowed amount of time you agree on with your parents, and keep an alarm clock on your desk. Many computers even have built-in alarms that you can program to go off when you want them to. Check your computer's manual to learn how to do this. Have a plan for what you're going to do before you go online. It will save you a lot of time. Some e-mail and newsreader programs let you download messages and articles onto your computer's hard drive. Afterward, when you're offline, you can read and respond to them, so you don't use up your online time.

5. EXPRESS YOURSELF, BUT STAY COOL.

It doesn't take too long to discover that there are people

Remember that you're in control when you're online. You can always log off if someone starts giving you a hard time.

whose only purpose in posting messages in Newsgroups seems to be to insult others or put them down. It's okay to complain about stuff you don't like, or to have a disagreement with a fellow Internaut. But don't let it get insulting and personal. As you have learned, that's called *flaming*, and it's no fun to get flamed. So don't you become a flamer!

6. IT'S OKAY TO BE A NEWBIE.

The Internet is so big and so complicated that it can be very confusing to the newcomer. It takes time to figure out how to reply to a message, engage in a chat, or just find your way around. If you're a newbie, someone on the Net will help you as well. No question is dumb if you don't know the answer. And remember, everybody was a newbie once!

7. USE YOUR COMMON SENSE.

One of the best things about being online is that if you ask a question on almost any topic you are sure to get five answers within an hour of posting your question. The problem is, three of the answers are likely to be wrong. This is not to say that you can't get help, just that you have to judge the quality of the help you get. You have to sort through the information to figure out what is true, what is valuable, and what's right for you. Everybody has an answer, but not everyone always knows what they're talking about.

8. ONLINE PEOPLE ARE REAL PEOPLE.

If you say something mean or hurtful in real life, you can expect that person to react, just as you would if someone said something nasty to you. If someone makes you angry online, take a minute and think before blurting out a response. Remember, there's a real person behind that user name.

9. SHARE IDEAS, SHARE FILES, SHARE YOURSELF.

The online world is full of people who are eager to share their information, time, and energy with others. Remember, you have ideas and information to share with others. Don't be shy! Share them. Maybe you just saw a great movie and think other people ought to see it. Post a message about it. This is what makes the cyberspace universe such a great place to be. There is a lot of **freeware** out there for the taking. And if you do find a program that's particularly useful, it's nice to drop an e-mail to the person who wrote it saying how helpful their program is.

10. CYBERSPACE CAN BE WHATEVER YOU WANT IT TO BE.

This doesn't mean you can ignore what the other Internauts are doing. Remember that we're all navigating through cyberspace together. But it does mean that you have to take part in making the Internet the kind of place you want to hang out in.

If you don't find a newsgroup that covers an area you're interested in, suggest a new one! If you think your school should have a World Wide Web page, as so many schools already do, talk to your teacher, and offer to help create one for your school.

Finally, remember that the Internet is like no other place in the known universe. It's a place that's being created as we go. There are plenty of things for kids to do here, and you can contribute. Think of it as your ticket to the 21st Century. You're way ahead of the game!

FREEWARE

Freeware is software that you use and give to your friends without paying for it—and it's okay to share it for free!

SHAREWARE

Shareware simply means that the software can be shared, but it must be paid for. You will come across a lot of software available to the public, but you will need a credit card to make the purchase.

"We will contribute," promises Kate.

"We sure will," Zack agrees. "The Internet is such a great place. We can make it even greater."

"Good," says CyberSarge. "Now get a good night's sleep. Tomorrow is a really big day!"

The next afternoon, Zack and Kate hurry into the room and switch on their computer. They wriggle anxiously in their seats. This is their big day. Today they graduate from Cyberspace Academy! They're going to advance from being Cadets to becoming full-fledged Internauts!

"All right, kids, sit up straight," says CyberSarge. "This is the moment you've been waiting for. Are you sure you're ready?"

"We're ready!" Zack and Kate reply, sitting up straighter in their chairs.

CyberSarge begins the Cyberspace Academy oath: "Do you swear to obey the Top Ten Rules of Surfing the Net, and treat your fellow Internauts as you want to be treated?"

"We do!" reply the kids.

"Do you promise not to spend more than the agreed-upon time in cyberspace each week, no matter how much fun you're having?" CyberSarge raises an eyebrow.

Ooh, that's a tough one. But Zack and Kate agree. "We promise."

CyberSarge stands straight and tall as he continues: "You both have completed all the requirements for promotion from Cadets to Internauts. And you have demonstrated the responsibility required of Internet voyagers. Therefore, by the authority vested in me as First Sergeant of Cyberspace Academy, I hereby pronounce you, Kate, and you, Zack . . . full-fledged Internauts!"

"All right!" Zack and Kate shout—causing their mother downstairs to call up: "Is everything okay?"

"We're fine, Mom," Kate replies, grinning at her brother.

They turn back to the screen—and it is blank! CyberSarge is gone!

"CyberSarge! Where are you?" Zack calls, tapping the *Enter* key on the keyboard.

"It's time for me to leave," comes CyberSarge's voice from the computer. "You two are ready to travel through cyberspace on your own."

"You can't leave!" Zack says. "What if we need you?"

"You know all you need to know about traveling the Internet," CyberSarge replies. "Besides, I've got more Cadets to train. But I'll be around if you really need me."

"How do we know where to go? Or how to get there?" Kate asks. "What if we get lost?"

"You have more help than you could possibly need," replies CyberSarge. "Remember, the Internet is filled with folks who love to help. Why, I'll bet that before long, you'll be the ones answering questions from some newbies. And you have this book as your manual."

CyberSarge appears again and salutes them. "Congratulations, Zack and Kate."

Kate and Zack are surprised, and a little bit nervous, as they salute back. "Well—see ya, CyberSarge," Zack says, sounding a little unsure.

"Thanks again for everything!" he remembers to add.

"What do we do now?" Kate asks.

On the screen, CyberSarge begins to fade from view. "I'll send a list of places to start exploring. You'll get a few more screen messages from me throughout this book, but from now on you're on your own! Have fun!"

Chapter 6
Getting Outfitted

We've talked a lot about the things you'll need to become an Internaut. Now, to make it easy for you, CyberSarge has put all the tools you might want in this special tool kit. Use his tool kit whenever you need reminders of what you've learned.

You know you need a computer, software, and a modem to go online, but you also need a gateway. A gateway is like Alice's looking glass: Step through and you're in the wonderland of the Internet. In this case, your gateway might be called a "linking glass" that connects your computer to the Internet.

There are two kinds of gateways you can select: commercial services or Internet service providers (ISP.) Each will get you on the Internet, but they take slightly different routes. Which route is best for you is something you'll have to decide. But we'll try to give you some information to make that choice easier.

Note that this information is, like the Internet, in a state of constant change. At this moment almost every ISP is offering unlimited access for $19.95 a month. Most providers also offer online storage space so you can create your own personal Web page.

COMMERCIAL SERVICES

Commercial online services are like little communities in cyberspace. They offer a friendly, easy-to-get-around way to explore the mysteries of the online world, and can be a good choice for newbies to explore this vast new universe.

These online services might be considered "value-added options," since the Big Four commercial services—America Online, CompuServe, Prodigy and Microsoft Network—give you a lot of extras in addition to the Internet. It used to be that a commercial service was a lot more expensive than an ISP, but that's no longer the case. You can pretty much figure that it will cost about twenty dollars a month for basic, full-time connection.

Commercial services provide two things that are worth considering, especially if this is your first time on the Internet:

1. **THEY'RE REALLY EASY TO SET UP AND USE**. You'll get **floppy disks** (or a CD-ROM), and the setup program will do everything for you pretty easily. Once you're connected to the service, you'll find friendly menus and icons that will make it simple to navigate.

2. **THEY HAVE A LOT OF EXTRAS**. There are games, magazines, reference databases, and other features that you can get only on that particular service.

FLOPPY DISK

A floppy disk is a small flexible plastic disk that is inserted into a computer's external disk drive and used to transfer or store information.

Who: AMERICA ONLINE

Where: *http://www.aol.com* or *800-827-6364*

What: AOL is the most popular commercial service, or at least it has the most subscribers. It's a friendly, well organized place that includes a lot of extras, like online chat rooms, entertainment information, and encyclopedias and dictionaries for helping with your homework. And there's a site just for kids, too. AOL has more than 1,000 local access numbers all over the United States. And while the traffic can be heavy here, it's still a good place for beginners to get their feet wet in cyberspace.

Who: COMPUSERVE

Where: *http://www.compuserve.com* or *800-848-8199*

What: The granddaddy of online services, CompuServe has many of the same features as AOL, and has always been a great resource for computer stuff. It doesn't have a special kids' area, but there are lots of special-interest groups (they call them SIGs) that are educational and entertaining. Phone and mail support are available every day twenty-four hours a day. There are 600-plus local access numbers, including a lot of overseas connections just in case you leave the country and can't live without your e-mail.

CYBERSARGE SAYS:

You can design a Web page of your own and also run your own programs. For instance, if your hobbies are sports and trivia, your Web page may contain a trivia program and an updated scoreboard of sports scores. Most of the national ISPs, and a lot of the local ones, will give you space for your own Web page. Just ask them if they provide that service before you sign up with them.

Who: PRODIGY
Where: *http://www.prodigy.com* or *800-PRODIGY*
What: Prodigy is the home of the homework helper and has a special home and family section. It also has lots of original content, with all the regular Internet features except for chat. There are 600 local access numbers, and phone and e-mail support.

Who: MICROSOFT NETWORK
Where: *http://www.msn.com* or *800-386-5550*
What: MSN is the new kid on the online services block. It has already undergone a major facelift and has added lots of new features, including a whole new kids' section that has games and online shows. This is the official Internet home of Star Trek. There are more than 800 local access numbers in many countries. Phone support is limited to 7 a.m. to 2 a.m. on the East Coast, but the number is toll free.

INTERNET SERVICE PROVIDERS

Getting Internet service from a provider used to be much more difficult than it is today, but now, like the commercial services, the national ISPs will usually give you an installation disk that includes a dialer program and a Web browser.

Who: NETCOM
Where: *http://www.netcom.com* or *800-353-6600*
What: One of the first national ISPs, Netcom also offers a personal news feature that e-mails a summary of different stories (sports, world

events, movies, etc.) to you every morning. Telephone support is available twenty-four hours a day, but it is not toll free.

Who: EARTHLINK
Where: *http://www.earthlink.net* or *800-393-8425*
What: Earthlink has grown from a regional southern California ISP to a national provider, with more than 300 local access numbers. For the regular $19.95 unlimited access fee, they'll throw in two megabytes of storage for your own personal Web page.

Who: AT&T WORLD NET
Where: *http://www.worldnet.att.net/* or *800-967-5363*
What: World Net charges a $19.95 flat fee if you're an AT&T long-distance user, otherwise, it's $24.95. There is no real original content, but there are 200 local access numbers and an 800 number you can use when you're in a town without an access number. They also provide a software bundle that includes Netscape Navigator.

Who: GTE INTERNET SOLUTIONS
Where: *http://www.gte.com* or *800-363-8483*
What: GTE provides 800 local access numbers and full-time, toll-free support. The unlimited-use fee is the standard $19.95, but there is only 1 megabyte of disk storage. CNET, a Web site that has its members rate their service provider, has given this one high marks.

CYBERSARGE SAYS:

Beware the 800 access numbers that most national ISPs provide. They can charge a "facility fee" of $4.00 to $6.00 per hour.

CYBERSARGE SAYS:

Confused about which ISP to choose?

Check out CNET at http://www.cnet.com *to get the latest facts on the ISP you're considering, and find out how their current users rate the service. CNET CENTRAL also reviews hardware, software, and games. It also offers shareware.*

Who: SPRYNET
Where: *http://www.sprynet.com* or *206-957-8997*
What: CompuServe's SpryNet has about 500 local access numbers. It offers live local and national concerts as a special attraction. In addition to the regular support, you can get help here via online chat.

Who: MINDSPRING
Where: *http://www.mindspring.com* or *800-719-4332*
What: MindSpring has become one of the largest national ISPs, with more than 235 local access numbers. You get the usual limited access for $19.95, or you pay $26.95 for ten megabytes of online storage space and multiple e-mail boxes.

These are most of the national providers. Remember though, there are also thousands of regional and local providers. The costs are about the same and sometimes the help service is even better. It's impossible to list them all, but they're not hard to find. Look in the phone book, newspaper, local giveaway computer magazines, and ask your friends.

If you're already online and looking to change your provider, check out The List.

Who: THE LIST
Where: *http://thelist.iworld.com/*
What: Here's the most complete list available of Internet service providers in the United States and Canada.

GETTING ORGANIZED

Now that you're online, you'll need software that will help you do exciting things on the Internet. Here are some suggestions from CyberSarge on what you may want.

WEB BROWSERS

Web browsers give you graphical pages, let you navigate the World Wide Web, and can also access data from Gophers, FTP, and Telnet applications.

CYBERSARGE SAYS:

The best online supermarket for browsing through shareware and freeware programs is:
    http://www.tucows.com

What is it? NETSCAPE NAVIGATOR

Why do I want it? Netscape Navigator is the most popular Web browser around—for good reason. It has its own e-mail, news, and FTP built-in programs.

Where do I get it? ***http://home.netscape.com***

What is it? MICROSOFT INTERNET EXPLORER

Why do I want it? Microsoft came to the Internet late, but since it has arrived it has become better with every new version. Like Navigator, Internet Explorer comes loaded with e-mail, newsgroups, chat, and other add-ins.

Where do I get it? ***http://www.microsoft.com/ie/***

What is it? ARIADNA

Why do I want it? Just in case you're interested, Ariadna is a new Web

CYBERSARGE SAYS:

A quick word here about Java. Programs written in this format can produce full-scale multimedia experiences including moving pictures, sound, and music on your desktop. There is no Java plug-in you need to down-load, you just need Netscape or Microsoft's current Web browsers—version 3.0 or later.

browser from Russia. It's not as sophisticated as its American cousins, but it reminds us that the Internet is a worldwide phenomenon.

Where do I get it? *http://www.amsd.ru/*

PLUG-INS

Plug-ins are software programs that extend the capability of your Web browser. For example, they let you play audio samples or view movie clips. Software companies are developing new plug-ins at a phenomenal rate, so keep looking for new ones. Here is a sampling of some of the plug-ins currently available, and where they can be downloaded.

What is it? QUICKTIME PLUG-IN FROM APPLE

Why do I want it? The QuickTime plug-in lets you view animation, movie, music, and audio files directly on your Web page. This is one of the more popular multimedia formats, and newer versions can even let you view a film clip as it is downloading.

Where do I get it? *http://www.quickTime.apple.com*

What is it? SHOCKWAVE

Why do I want it? Shockwave is a multimedia player that plays a wide variety of multimedia content, from animation and interactive games to streaming audio and live concerts. This plug-in works with all leading Web browsers.

Where do I get it? ***http://www.macromedia.com /shockwave/***

What is it? NETSCAPE MEDIA PLAYER

Why do I want it? This media player brings high-quality streaming audio and multimedia to your desktop. This has become one of the most popular audio features. With this plug-in you can listen to radio stations, news broadcasts, and even old-time radio programs.

Where do I get it? ***http://home.mcom.com***

What is it? ACROBAT AMBER

Why do I want it? This plug-in allows you to read PDF files from within your Web browser. PDF files are documents that have graphics and special fonts.

Where do I get it? ***http://www.adobe.com/Amber***

What is it? COOL-TALK PLUG-IN FOR NETSCAPE

Why do I want it? Cool-Talk is a real-time audio and data plug-in specifically designed for the Internet that lets you talk in special chat rooms.

Where do I get it? ***http://www.netscape.com***

What is it?   REALAUDIO

Why do I want it?   RealAudio provides live and on-demand real-time audio on the Internet. There are lots of RealAudio sites, where you can listen to music, or listen to sports events—live and online.

Where do I get it?   *http://www.realaudio.com*

What is it?   ICHAT PLUG-IN

Why do I want it?   Ichat was one of the first plug-ins to integrate chat capabilities directly into your Web browser. Whenever you open an IRC page, ichat opens a window in the lower part of the browser window. Within that frame, ichat displays a real-time, ongoing chat session among all the visitors to the Web page. Visitors can communicate with one another while continuing to browse the Web.

Where do I get it?   *http://www.ichat.com*

What is it?   EARTHTIME

Why do I want it?   This plug-in lets you know the time anywhere around the world.

Where do I get it?   *http://www.starfishsoftware .com*

HELPER APPLICATIONS

While plug-ins are considered add-ins and work within your Web browser, helper applications are stand-alone programs that aren't part of your Web browser. But like plug-ins, helper applications work to extend the capabilities of your browser. For example, some of them can download Web pages for offline reading, or organize your bookmarks.

Here are just a few that CyberSarge likes:

What is it?	BROWSER BUDDY FOR WINDOWS
Why do I want it?	This is a program that fetches Web pages from the Internet and stores them on your hard drive so you can browse them offline later.
Where do I get it?	*http://www.softbots.com*

What is it?	CYBERPATROL
Why do I want it?	CyberPatrol allows you to manage and limit computer use and online access.
Where do I get it?	*http://www.cyberpatrol.com*

What is it?	OIL CHANGE
Why do I want it?	This handy utility checks the Internet to keep track of new versions of many of your programs and can update them automatically.
Where do I get it?	*http://www.cybermedia.com*

What is it?	QUIKLINK EXPLORER
Why do I want it?	QuikLink Explorer is a utility

program that lets you organize all your bookmarks and favorites, from all sources, into a single, easy-to-manage file. Then you can use this list to launch your Web browser and go directly to the chosen site.

Where do I get it?   ***http://www.quiklinks.com***

What is it?   UNMOZIFY
Why do I want it?   UnMozify allows you to selectively retrieve files from Netscape's cache for offline viewing. With UnMozify, you can look at your favorite Web pages without having to go back online.
Where do I get it?   ***http://www.evolve.co.uk /unmozify***

What is it?   WEBWACKER
Why do I want it?   WebWacker downloads single Web pages or entire Web sites and stores a complete copy on your computer.
Where do I get it?   ***http://www.ffg.com/wacker .html***

UTILITIES

Utilities are stand-alone programs that can do things your Web browser doesn't do, or does poorly. Most of these are small shareware programs (which don't cost much) and normally you can download a trial version to see if it's what you want. We've included a few of our favorite utilities here.

E-MAIL APPLICATIONS

E-mail lets you send messages from one computer to another. Your ISP acts like a post office, and these programs are like the letter carriers who deliver and collect your mail. Although most ISPs and commercial services have excellent e-mail functions, we've listed a stand-alone program for your reference.

What is it? EUDORA LIGHT

Why do I want it? This is the freeware version of what is probably the best stand-alone e-mail program available.

Where do I get it? *http://www.eudora.com*

NEWSREADERS

Newsreaders allow you to access Usenet newsgroups so you can define which groups you want to pick.

What is it? FREE AGENT

Why do I want it? This is the freeware version of Agent, one of the best newsreaders. You can select newsgroups, mark message headers for retrieval, and then read the messages offline.

Where do I get it? *http://www.forteinc.com/forte*

What is it? WINVN

Why do I want it? WinVn was one of the first newsreader programs and still a good choice. Plus, it's easy to set up and use.

Where do I get it? *http://www.ksc.nasa.gov/ software/winvn/winvn.html*

DESKTOP

Your desktop is what you see and keep on your computer screen. It's the same as your desk at home or in school, where you might keep pens, pencils, paper, and books. These are tools that help you work by hand. Your computer desktop might contain icons that give you direct access to programs in your computer. They are the main tools to help you work your computer.

What is it?   INTERNEWS

Why do I want it?   Internews is a newsreader designed specifically for you Mac users.

Where do I get it?   *http://www.dartmouth.edu/~moonrise/*

NEWS SERVICES

News services are online services that deliver a variety of news and information right to your **desktop**.

What is it?   MY YAHOO! NEWS TICKER

Why do I want it?   News Ticker is your own personal organizer and custom launch pad on to the World Wide Web. Get the latest news, sports, and more, in the blink of an eye.

Where do I get it?   *http://www.netcontrols.com*

FTP

File Transfer Protocol is the way computers on the Internet exchange files. Although your Web browser can accomplish this, sometimes a stand-alone program is better if you're exchanging a lot of files.

What is it?   NETLOAD

Why do I want it?   Netload is a file-transfer system that talks to conventional FTP servers and is smart enough to upload only those files that are new and updated.

Where do I get it? ***http://www.aerosoft.com.au/
netload/***

What is it? WS-FTP
Why do I want it? WS-FTP is a great application
that allows you to transfer
and edit files on a remote
computer.
Where do I get it? ***http://www.ipswitch.com/pd_
wsftp.html***

ARCHIE

Archie is a giant database of all the files that are
known to be available by FTP. With an Archie
program you can search for a file, get a list of the
FTP sites that have that file, then use FTP to
download it later.

What is it? FTPARCHIE
Why do I want it? Probably the best Archie
program around, FTPArchie
comes with a built-in FTP
program.
Where do I get it? ***http://www.fpware.demon.nl/***

What is it? WS-ARCHIE
Why do I want it? WS-Archie is another good
Archie program for locating
files.
Where do I get it? ***http://dspace.dial.pipex.com/
town/square/cc83/***

INTERNET RELAY CHAT

IRC allows users on different computers to chat with one another in chat rooms.

What is it?   ACTIVE WORLDS EXPLORER

Why do I want it?   Formerly known as Alpha World, this is a real-time chat software program that can be used from the Web.

Where do I get it?   *http://www.worlds.net/alpha world/*

What is it?   GLOBAL CHAT FOR WINDOWS

Why do I want it?   Global Chat has live chatting rooms with different subjects. You can pick and choose which subjects interest you.

Where do I get it?   *http://www.qdeck.com/chat/*

What is it?   INTERNET TELE-CAFE

Why do I want it?   This chat system has grown to become one of the largest online chat systems, with 20,000 members. You can meet people from all around the world.

Where do I get it?   *http://www.telecafe.com/tele cafe/*

What is it?   MICROSOFT COMIC CHAT FOR WINDOWS

Why do I want it?   Comic Chat is a new kind of graphical chat program. As you type in text, a comic strip unfolds showing everybody who's chatting in the conversation as comic characters and what they're saying in word balloons. Holy cow! I'm in a comic book on the Web!

Where do I get it? ***http://www.microsoft.com/ie/comichat/***

VOICE CHAT

Tired of typing? These programs will let you participate in real-time voice communication over the Internet. It's talking IRC. However, you'll need a microphone attached to your computer's **sound card** or **voice modem**.

What is it? INTERPHONE

Why do I want it? InterPhone has a very nice graphic interface and the ability to leave messages in an answering-machine format. You contact other InterPhone users through their user names or through a built-in phone book.

Where do I get it? ***http://www.interphone.com***

What is it? POW WOW

Why do I want it? Pow Wow allows up to seven people to chat via keyboard or voice, travel to Web pages together, exchange files and

SOUND CARD

A sound card is a piece of hardware inside your computer that will play sounds when connected to speakers.

VOICE MODEM

A voice modem is simply a modem with a microphone attached to it. You will be able to speak into it and you will also be able to hear sound.

pictures, and play sounds.

Where do I get it? *http://www.tribal.com*

MOVIE VIEWERS

Movie Viewers are applications that allow you to view movie files in different formats, such as QuickTime, MPEG, or Microsoft AVI.

What is it? NET TOOB

Why do I want it? Net Toob is one of the best multimedia viewers.

Where do I get it? *http://www.duplexx.com*

What is it? QUICKTIME PLAYER

Why do I want it? This is a software program created by Apple used to play multimedia files—text, audio, and video—over the Internet.

Where do I get it? *http://quickTime.apple.com/*

What is it? QUICKTIME VR PLAYER

Why do I want it? This is Apple's QuickTime VR player that allows you to experience virtual reality on your computer.

Where do I get it? *http://quickTime.apple.com/*

What is it? POINTCAST

Why do I want it? This is a complete integrated news, weather, sports, and news package that brings the latest stories right to your desktop.

Where do I get it? *http://www.pointcast.com*

AUDIO APPLICATIONS

Audio applications are programs that let you listen to and record music and sounds.

What is it? REALAUDIO PLAYER

Why do I want it? RealAudio allows you to listen to streaming audio that plays in real-time while you're browsing the Web. You can also download RealAudio files (*.ra*) to listen offline.

Where do I get it? *http://www.realaudio.com*

What is it? TRUESPEECH

Why do I want it? Truespeech software enables the efficient compression, storage, and playback of digital speech.

Where do I get it? *http://www.dspg.com/*

INTERNET TOOLS

These are utilities that extend various tasks, like doing multiple searches using different search engines.

What is it? CU-SEEME

Why do I want it? CU-SeeMe allows video conferencing over the Internet, even at slower speeds. It includes video, audio, chat, and even a shared whiteboard you can write and draw on.

Where do I get it? *http://www.cu-seeme.com*

What is it?   INTERNET AGENTS

Why do I want it?   This handy tool makes things happen on your computer when you're not there. Your friendly agent can log on to your service, check your mail, visit Web pages for any changes, and find the latest news. (It still can't make your dinner though!)

Where do I get it?   *http://www.agents-tech.com*

What is it?   LOOK@ME

Why do I want it?   Look@Me is a freeware collaboration tool that allows you to edit documents, review graphics, and even watch what's happening on the remote computer of another Look@Me user.

Where do I get it?   *http://www.farallon.com*

What is it?   BYELINES

Why do I want it?   ByeLines makes it simple for you to create e-mail and newsgroup signature files. These are files that are automatically attached to your outgoing e-mail messages and postings to newsgroups.

Where do I get it?   *http://www.kyler.com/Bye Lines.html*

What is it?   WATCHDOG

Why do I want it?   This neat little tool keeps

track of how much time you spend on the computer.

Where do I get it? *http://www.geocities.com/TimesSquare/*

What is it? PKZIP

Why do I want it? PKZIP is a Windows utility for **compressing** and **decompressing** files. It squeezes your files smaller to make sending and receiving them faster. PKZIP also bunches several files into one file to make the files easy to send.

Where do I get it? *http://www.pkware.com*

What is it? STUFF-IT

Why do I want it? Stuff-It is the Macintosh equivalent of PKZIP.

Where do I get it? *http://www.apple.com*

What is it? WINZIP

Why do I want it? WINZIP is another very good compression/decompression utility program.

Where do I get it? *http://www.winzip.com*

What is it? WINWEATHER

Why do I want it? WinWeather displays hourly weather reports and forecasts.

Where do I get it? *http://www.igsnet.com/igs*

What is it? WEBSEEK

Why do I want it? This utility allows you to

conduct Web searches from your desktop, without having to load a search form, which you find in search engine programs.

Where do I get it? *http://www.personal.umich.edu/~jeffhu/webseek*

What is it? WEBSEEKER

Why do I want it? WebSeeker runs your search question or key word through more than twenty Internet search engines.

Where do I get it? *http://www.ffg.com/seeker.html*

What is it? NETSCAN

Why do I want it? Just because you're accessing a Web site on another part of the Internet doesn't mean the information is coming directly from there to you. Like a ping pong ball, the information may bounce off a lot of different ports before it gets to you. This neat program will let you check the route, including detours, your information is taking.

Where do I get it? *http://www.eskimo.com/~nwps/nstmain.html*

What is it? MCAFEE VIRUSCAN

Why do I want it? This is an excellent virus scanner that checks all areas

COMPRESSION

Compression makes computer files smaller, so that less room is needed to contain the same amount of information.

DECOMPRESSION

Decompression returns compressed files to their natural size so that the information or data in the files can be used.

of your computer for potential viruses.

Where do I get it? ***http://www.mcafee.com/***

What is it? NORTON ANTI-VIRUS

Why do I want it? Norton's excellent anti-virus program is often updated. You can also install it into Netscape as a plug-in to check your downloads before saving them to your computer.

Where do I get it? ***http://www.symantec.com /avcenter/index.html***

What is it? LVIEW PRO

Why do I want it? Lview is a great image file editor that lets you view, save, and edit image files in the standard Internet graphics formats.

Where do I get it? ***http://world.std.com/~ mmedia/lviewp.html***

GAMES AND OTHER ENTERTAINMENT

The Internet is not just about looking for information to help you with your homework! There are a lot of online games and sources of entertainment for your recreation. Many of them will allow you to interact with one or more individuals.

What is it? CHESSMASTER ONLINE

Why do I want it? The famous computer game is

now online. Play against other users all over the world!

Where do I get it?   ***http://www.chessmaster.com***

What is it?   NET TRIVIA

Why do I want it?   This online database of trivia has thousands of questions for the inquiring mind. You can even add your own. Challenge your mind and try it for a free trial period.

Where do I get it?   ***http://www.nettrivia.com/ nettrivia/***

What is it?   NETCHECKERS

Why do I want it?   This is an Internet checkers game. Players can connect using the Net addresses of other players.

Where do I get it?   ***http://www.pillarsoft.com/***

What is it?   PUEBLO INTERNET GAME SYSTEM

Why do I want it?   Pueblo is a network game system that brings you together with other fun-loving kids on the Internet. The Pueblo folks believe that if you can bring different cultures, ages, and backgrounds together on the Internet, the world will be a much nicer place.

Where do I get it?   ***http://www.chaco.com/ pueblo/***

What is it?	INETRIS
Why do I want it?	Inetris is a Tetris game that you can play alone or with up to eight other Internet players.
Where do I get it?	*http://www.dur.ac.uk/~d405 ua/*

What is it?	QUAKE
Why do I want it?	From the folks who gave you Doom, Quake is a popular multi-user game. You can play Quake in single-user mode or against other players on the Internet.
Where do I get it?	*http://www.idsoftware.com/*

What is it?	SGH'S BATTLESHIP
Why do I want it?	BattleShip is a competitive game for two players. You challenge other Internet users located anywhere in the world.
Where do I get it?	*http://www.sgh-hive.com/ Battle.htm*

What is it?	HOVER RACE
Why do I want it?	Hover Race is a cool online game where you race bumper car–like hover cars against other drivers on the Internet. There is an online meeting room where you can join races, chat, and talk to one another.
Where do I get it?	*http://www.grokksoft.com/*

What is it? SUBSPACE FOR WINDOWS

Why do I want it? SubSpace is a shoot-em-up space game played entirely over the Internet against live opponents.

Where do I get it? *http://www.vie.com/sniper/*

What is it? WORLD EMPIRE

Why do I want it? World Empire IV is the latest installment (at the moment) of this popular strategy game. Play with up to seven other players live on the Internet.

Where do I get it? *http://viablesoftware.com/empireiv/index.htm*

What is it? ZMUD

Why do I want it? zMUD allows you to connect to and play MUDs on the Internet. It provides several tools—aliases, actions, macros, scripts—to make your MUD life easier and more fun.

Where do I get it? *http://www.trail.com/~zugg/*

Chapter 7

Guide to the Galaxy:

Cool Places to Surf on the Net

The next day, when Kate and Zack return to their computer, they find one last message from CyberSarge waiting on the screen:

File	Edit	View

MESSAGE FROM CYBERSARGE TO ALL INTERNAUTS

All right, Internauts, you've learned the ins and outs of your spacecraft, traveled to a few places, and talked with people from all over the world with me as your guide.

Now it's time for you to begin your solo voyages into

CYBERSARGE'S GALACTIC HOTSPOTS

1. COMMUNICATING

Here are some places for you to communicate with other kids and read what other kids have to say.

2. EXPLORING

From the Paris subway to the moon to the inside of a volcano or the inside of a human body, here are just some of the places you can discover.

3. FINDING

With the millions of Web sites out there on the Net, where do you start? Here are some jumping-off points for your voyage around the Internet.

4. LEARNING

Here's where to go to get help for your math homework, solve a computer problem, or see what kids at other schools are doing online.

5. PLAYING

Here's some of the fun stuff, like virtual reality sites, mysteries, magic, and playing and watching sports.

the vast reaches of the Internet. You won't need a map, though. What you will need is a way to find the places you're looking for. In the two years since the first edition of *Internet for Kids* was published, the World Wide Web has grown at a fantastic rate. In 1995 there were about 40,000 active Web sites on the Internet. Now there are millions!

Whatever you're looking for, you'll almost certainly find it out there on the Internet.

In this new edition of *Internet for Kids*, you'll find many new and exciting sites for you to visit, and to get you started, here's a list of galactic hot spots. It's important to remember that the Internet is constantly changing and some of the places you pick to visit might not be there anymore. But that's okay. With so many new sites going online each day, you're sure to find something else that's just as interesting. Ready? Here we go! The list is divided into five useful categories.

1. COMMUNICATING

There Are People To Meet

These are some interesting places where you can find out about people and places from all around the world.

Who: KIDS ON THE WEB
Where: *http://www.zen.org/~brendan/kids.html*
What: This is a well-maintained list of sites that offer information for and about kids. Among other things, it includes a lot of stuff to play with and information about education and schools from kindergarten to high school.

Who: A GIRL'S WORLD

Where: *http://www.agirlsworld.com/*

What: A Girl's World is an online clubhouse for girls. Your hosts, Amy, Rachel, Geri, and Tessa, invite you to explore their clubhouse. See what's hot! Check out Winter Carnival! Make friends with pen pals! Read Amy's Secret Diary! Meet incredible women. Create fun stuff. Amaze your friends with fun facts and features.

Who: LIENA'S COZY LITTLE PLACE IN CYBERSPACE

Where: *http://www.angelfire.com/free/myhome page.html*

What: Liena is eleven and has lots of interesting links on her home page.

Who: PATHFINDER MUSIC

Where: *http://pathfinder.com/@@ko67NgYAU JbBYVjo/music/*

What: Pathfinder is a great source for music videos and clips. Bush, Dr. Dre, Whitney Houston, and The Wallflowers are among the groups featured. You can also find music business gossip, album reviews, and interviews here.

Who: E-MAIL ADDRESSES FOR U.S. SENATORS

Where: *http://iecc.com/senate.html*

What: Get involved in politics—right from your home! Here's where you can write to your senator, who will be listed alphabetically by state.

CYBERSARGE SAYS:

Some Web sites are great because of what they contain, but others will become favorites because they are springboards to dozens of other sites.

Who: E-MAIL ADDRESSES FOR MEMBERS OF THE HOUSE OF REPRESENTATIVES

Where: *http://iecc.com/house.html*

What: Find your congressperson on the Internet, listed alphabetically by state.

PLACES TO VISIT

Who: THE YUCKIEST SITE ON THE INTERNET

Where: *http://www.nj.com/yucky/index.html*

What: If you're into really yucky things like worms and roaches, then this site was made for you!

Who: WORLDS CHAT

Where: *http://205.153.208.59/wcg/wcg-about.html*

What: Worlds Chat is a 3-D social environment where you can explore individual rooms on a virtual reality space station. This was one of the first of the avatar-based online environments, and is still one of the best. But, you'll have to download the special software before you play.

Who: THE PALACE

Where: *http://www.thepalace.com/index.html*

What: The Palace is like an audience-participation play that keeps evolving. When you first log on, you'll find yourself in a huge mansion with countless rooms, all of which are wonderfully decorated and tantalizingly complex. Many different Palace sites exist, but they all require you to download and run their special software first.

IDEAS TO EXCHANGE

Who: CYBERKIDS

Where: *http://www.cyberkids.com*

What: CyberKids is an online newsletter featuring kids' writing and art, sponsored by Mountain Lake Software. Post your stories and artwork here, explore the Web, or find a cyberpal. It's a free site, and all kinds of goodies are yours for the clicking once you fill out the online registration form. With loads of exciting new content every week, it's a great launch pad for young Internauts.

Who: ISN KIDNEWS

Where: *http://www.vsa.cape.com/~powens/Kidnews.html*

What: ISN KidNews is an online newspaper that accepts submissions from kids all over the world. Participation from schools and individuals is strongly encouraged.

Who: KIDZ MAGAZINE ON-LINE

Where: *http://www.TheTemple.com/Kidz Magazine/*

What: Want the latest news on upcoming video games? Want to know what other kids think about the latest books, movies, TV shows, and CDs? Want to read stories written by kids? You'll find it all at Kidz Magazine On-line.

Who: LITTLE PLANET TIMES

Where: *http://www.littleplanet.com/*

What: Each week, Little Planet Times presents

CYBERSARGE SAYS:

Remember, whenever you see a URL address that takes up more than one line in this book, like:

http://www.unitedstates ofamerica.com/mystate/ mycity/mystreet.html

It should be typed out as one continuous line, with no space where the line breaks. There are never any spaces in Internet addresses.

CYBERSARGE SAYS:

Sometimes you'll go to a Web page that should have what you're looking for, but it's so big and rambling that you can't find the item. Well, both Navigator and Explorer will search the page itself. Click on the Edit *menu, then click on* Find. *Now enter the text you're looking for, and click on* Find Next *to get there. Once there, the word will be highlighted.*

kids with a moral problem. In one recent issue, Happypotamus wondered if he should tell his friends he saw a prehistoric creature and risk being laughed at, or keep it to himself. Kids are encouraged to send in their own answers and maybe learn something along the way.

Who: K.I.D.S.: KIDS IDENTIFYING AND DISCOVERING SITES

Where: *http://wwwscout.cs.wisc.edu/scout/KIDS/index.html*

What: K.I.D.S., a publication produced by students in kindergarten through twelfth grade, was designed to help other students. It is an ongoing, cooperative effort of two classrooms in the Madison Metropolitan School District (Madison, Wisconsin), and two classrooms in the Boulder Valley School District (Boulder, Colorado). Teachers assist and provide support; however, students select and annotate all resources included in every issue of K.I.D.S.

Who: CHILDREN'S EXPRESS

Where: *http://www.ce.org/*

What: This is another Web site that is researched, written, and edited by children for everyone to enjoy. Children's Express is an organization dedicated to voicing children's and teens' concerns.

2. EXPLORING

These are sites that will take you to places you've never been, and let you see things that you have seen before in a whole new way.

Let's Go Traveling To Faraway Places

Who: USA CITYLINK
Where: *http://usacitylink.com/*
What: The USA CityLink project is the most comprehensive United States city and state listing on the Web, as well as one of the most visited sites on the Internet today. It provides users with a starting point when accessing information about U.S. states and cities. State home pages, city pages, CityLink pages, and freenet home pages are listed here.

Who: SOCKS WHITE HOUSE TOUR
Where: *http://www.whitehouse.gov/WH/kids /html/home.html*
What: Yes, Socks, the Clintons' cat, takes you on a virtual tour of the White House. If you want to learn about the children who've lived in the White House, or how many gallons of paint it takes to cover the outside, this is the site. You can send an e-mail message to the President or the Vice President—and get an answer!

Who: LE LOUVRE
Where: *http://mistral.enst.fr/~pioch/louvre/*
What: One of the most famous art museums in the world, France's Le Louvre is now

CYBERSARGE SAYS:

Since the Internet is global, you'll find lots of sites in more than one language. You might experiment by exploring some sites in a foreign language.

online as a virtual museum in cyberspace. There are paintings by Van Gogh, Cezanne, and other masters, and usually one or two special exhibits. This is a visual feast for the eyes for art lovers of all ages.

Who: SUBWAY NAVIGATOR
Where: *http://metro.jussieu.fr:10001/bin/cities/ english*
What: This Web site lets you check routes on subway systems all over the world. Current countries include Argentina, Austria, Belgium, Brazil, Canada, Chile, Czech Republic, Finland, France, Germany, Greece, Hong Kong, Hungary, India, Israel, Italy, Japan, Mexico, Netherlands, Norway, Poland, Russia, Singapore, and Venezuela. The word *english* at the end of the URL means the site language is English. Replace it with the word *french* for a French language version.

Who: MUNGO PARK
Where: *http://www.mungopark.com/*
What: Mungo Park is an online travel and exploration magazine covering current adventures, such as a trip up a South American river and a NASA shuttle flight. Other pages discuss the possibility of life on Mars and "Astronaut Chic," for what to wear in space. Past issues have discussed Mungo Park (yes, he was a real person!), who followed explorer Ann Jones in her search for a legendary Bantu tribe.

Who: THE ARCTIC CIRCLE
Where: *http://www.lib.uconn.edu/ArcticCircle/*
What: At this site, you'll discover the history, geography, culture, and environment of the very far North. But, of course, you won't be cold when you visit here!

Who: VIRTUAL GALAPAGOS
Where: *http://www.terraquest.com/galapagos/ intro.html*
What: Join the TerraQuest team in their virtual exploration of those fascinating islands— the Galapagos. Plenty of maps and pictures will make your trip educational as well as exciting.

Who: GLOBAL ONLINE ADVENTURE
Where: *http://www.goals.com/*
What: When John Oman left Seattle in November, 1995, to sail around the world on his sixty-foot yacht, he invited the rest of us to share the adventure. Read his logs, view his pictures, and become a virtual seafarer.

Who: THE ADVENTURE CHANNEL
Where: *http://www.180.com*
What: The Adventure Channel takes you on a virtual bicycle ride around Europe and lets you participate in climbing the highest mountains in North, South, and Central America without leaving your desk.

Who: ROADTRIP AMERICA
Where: *http://www.roadtripamerica.com*
What: These are the adventures of Mark, Megan, and Marvin the Road Dog on their continuing road trip across North America in their four-wheel motor home. See the back roads of America in a whole new way.

Who: RAINFOREST ACTION NETWORK
Where: *http://www.ran.org/ran/kids_action/index.html*
What: This great site focuses on what kids can do to help the environment. Topics include "What You Can Do," "Life in the Rainforests," "Kid's Art Gallery," "Resources for Teachers and Students," and "Rainforest Audio-visuals."

Who: E-PATROL
Where: *http://www.sprint.com/epatrol*
What: The E-Patrol Foundation is an independent, nonprofit organization created to help teach kids how to solve and prevent environmental problems. E-Patrollers are joining together to change the world.

Who: THE WHY FILES
Where: *http://whyfiles.news.wisc.edu*
What: If the X-Files leave you confused, then the Why Files will enlighten you on almost everything. And twice a month, the Why Files will take something from the headlines and explain it in terms even adults can understand.

Let's Discover Interesting Trivia

Who: ARISTOKIDS NEWSLETTER
Where: *http://intergalactic.com/aris.htm*
What: Aristoplay has a fun collection of educational games for kids to play with one another and their parents. There are quizzes, contests, and questions asked and answered in this entertaining and nicely designed interactive newsletter for kids.

Who: NET LINGO
Where: *www.netlingo.com*
What: Cyberbabble can be confusing, especially to fledgling Internauts. This Web site is a good place to help you talk the talk—so you can walk the walk.

3. FINDING

How do you find what you're looking for in this gigantic universe? If you don't know a particular site's address already, you can't—unless you use one of the search engines we mentioned before. These Internet tools listed below search the World Wide Web for sites, make a note of their contents, and keep a list of where they've been.

With millions of Web sites now on the Internet, and more arriving every day, it's impossible for you to find what you need by "just looking." That's why search engines were invented. They are the catalogs of the World Wide Web, keeping track (or trying to!) of the thousands of new pages that go up every day.

Some of the search engine companies employ people to sit at computers all day, traveling the Web to find new sites to add to their lists. Other sites use special software programs to cruise the World Wide Web and collect the information. Other search sites keep track of just the URLs or addresses, titles, and a few opening sentences of Web pages, and some gather all the information from sites they visit.

SO HOW DO I SEARCH?

1. **PICK THE RIGHT SEARCH ENGINE**. If you're looking for a general topic, a directory like Yahoo will probably give you enough information to get started. But if you need specific information about steam-powered automobiles, try one of the full-text search engines like Infoseek or AltaVista.

2. **USE ONE OF THE SPECIAL-INTEREST SEARCH ENGINES**. For example, finding information about Keanu Reaves will be much easier at the Internet Movie Database than at Yahoo.

3. **PUT QUOTE MARKS AND PARENTHESES AROUND PHRASES OR PROPER NAMES**. Searching for Web pages about a president by entering, let's say—*"(William Jefferson Clinton)"*—will avoid sites that mention William Randolph, Thomas Jefferson, and DeWitt Clinton.

4. **USE CAPITAL LETTERS IF YOU WANT AN EXACT CASE MATCH**. If you enter a keyword in lowercase, most search engines will find both uppercase and lowercase matches.

5. **USE LESS COMMON WORDS OR SYNONYMS TO NARROW YOUR SEARCH**. If you search using a word that is very general, like *business* you'll get an overwhelmingly long

list of results—sometimes you could get up to 20,000 references! The more specific you are, the narrower your list of results will be. For example, if you had a homework project in which you had to get information on business and the stockmarket, you would enter *Wall Street* or *stockmarket*.

CYBERSARGE SAYS:

Boolean operators are special words used to link your search words together so your search will go faster. **AND, OR, NOT** *are examples of Boolean operators.*

6. **USE MORE THAN ONE WORD**. For example, if you're looking for information about traveling in Africa, try entering the phrase *travel AND Africa. AND* is called a **Boolean** operator. It will deliver results that contain both of the words you enter (although they don't have to appear next to each other, as they do when you use quotation marks.) However, note that search engines such as AltaVista use the plus sign (+) instead of *AND*.

7. **USE THE BOOLEAN OPERATOR *NOT* (OR THE MINUS SYMBOL) TO EXCLUDE WORDS FROM A SEARCH QUERY**. Searching for *"lions AND tigers NOT zoo"* will focus your search on wild animals as opposed to caged ones in zoos.

8. **FIND VARIATIONS ON YOUR WORD BY USING THE ASTERISK (*) SYMBOL**. Using an asterisk (*) as part of a search word makes it a wildcard search. For example, starting your query with **ball* will deliver pages on football, baseball, and handball. [NOTE: Not all search sites support this.]

9. **ALL SEARCH SITES HAVE *HELP* PAGES**. Using them will shorten your searches and your time online.

WHERE DO I SEARCH?

Here is a list of a few major search engines to get you started.

QUERY

A query is another word for a question for a search site. Queries are often written in key words, but you can also type in phrases such as *lions AND tigers*.

Who: ALTAVISTA
Where: *http://www.altavista.digital.com/*
What: This is one of the better search engines on the World Wide Web. AltaVista searches other search engines, as well as Usenet newsgroups, and can do both simple and advanced searches. One neat thing about AltaVista is that after you've submitted a search, you can change your key words to generate new searches or to narrow down the responses to your current search. It also lists responses according to the relevance of your topic.

Who: EXCITE
Where: *http://excite.com*
What: Excite searches the World Wide Web, Usenet, Usenet classifieds, and Excite's own database of Web site reviews. While Excite will likely find the information you want, it isn't as powerful and detailed as some other search engines listed here. Excite lists search results according to how closely they match your query. You can also click on an icon for links to similar documents.

Who: INFOSEEK GUIDE
Where: *http://guide.infoseek.com/*
What: Infoseek Guide is another popular World Wide Web search engine. A major feature

of Infoseek's is its ability to search Usenet newsgroups and FTP sites. Like Yahoo, Infoseek also allows searches by topic, such as *sports*. However, Infoseek Guide is limited to providing only the first 100 matches to your query. If you want more, you (actually your parents) will have to sign up for the Infoseek Professional service, which costs money.

Who: INTERNET SLEUTH
Where: *http://www.isleuth.com/*
What: The Internet Sleuth is called a metasearch engine, which means that it searches other search engines (say that five times fast!). Type in a query and this engine will go dig up answers in Lycos, AltaVista, and others. It's also good at finding information on specific topics, like *electronics* or *early aviation*. One problem with the Sleuth is that you have to retype your query for each search engine (cutting and pasting helps here). Give this one a try if the other engines don't help.

Who: LYCOS
Where: *http://www.lycos.com*
What: Lycos is an easy-to-use, powerful tool for finding stuff on the Web. Type in your search key words, and Lycos delivers results in order of importance. For instance, if you want information on the famous aviatrix Amelia Earhart, Lycos will find references on her before it goes

looking for the word Amelia by itself. You
can also use Boolean operators such as
AND, as in *computers AND games*. One
problem with Lycos is that it excludes
certain common words such as *the*, *and*,
and *new* from its searches, so if you try to
perform a search on, say, *New England*,
Lycos will ignore the word *New* and
deliver a lot of information on *England*.

Who: MAGELLAN STELLAR SITES
Where: *http://www.mckinley.com/pick.cgi*
What: This is a surprise site because clicking here
        will bring you to Magellan's choice for an
        interesting site of the day. Dr. Shannon
        Lucid's record-breaking stay in space
        aboard the MIR station was most recently
        featured, along with links to other space-
        themed Web sites. Stellar Sites is like a
        pot-luck dinner on the Web. You never
        know what you're going to find!

Who: METACRAWLER
Where: *http://metacrawler.cs.washington.edu:
        8080/index.html*
What: Another metasearch engine (as you might
        guess from its name). MetaCrawler actually
        sends your query to other search engines
        and after it gets answers, it eliminates
        duplications! Pretty cool, huh? You can
        group words in quotes and parentheses if
        you want MetaCrawler to only look for
        them together. You can also set a time limit
        for your search. MetaCrawler is sometimes
        complicated to use, and the fact that it

searches so well means you have to
be patient when waiting for results.

Who: YAHOOLIGANS
Where: *www.yahooligans.com*
What: Yahooligans is a great Web search engine
for kid-oriented Web pages. It has lots of
advertising aimed at kids, but it's useful
because of what you can find. "Around
the World," "School Bell," "Homework
Answers," "Art Soup Museums,"
"Environment," "Dinosaurs,"
"Computers," "Games," "Online
Shareware," "Movies," "Music,"
"Magazines," "The Scoop," "Comics,"
and a "Yahooligans" newsletter are all
at this site.

Who: YAHOO
Where: *http://www.yahoo.com*
What: The "grown-up" version of Yahooligans,
Yahoo is one of the easiest search engines
to use if you have a pretty good idea of
what you're looking for. You search here
by category, such as entertainment, news,
or sports, and Yahoo only looks in its
own index, but it's a pretty big index. If
you need more detailed information,
though, there are better search engines.

Who: THE INTERNET KIDS
YELLOW PAGES
Where: *http://www.well.com/user/polly/ikyp.
html*

What: Based on the adult Internet Yellow Pages,
        this site has links and information about
        kid-related World Wide Web sites and
        activities.

FINDING MAILING LISTS

If you're searching for mailing lists that you might
want to subscribe to, here's a place to start:

Who: LISZT DIRECTORY OF E-MAIL
        MAILING LISTS
Where: *http://www.liszt.com/*
What: Want to join a Listserv discussion group?
        This is the place to start. At last count
        there were more than 67,000 lists from
        2,100 sites that you can search by
        category or key word.

FINDING NEWSGROUPS

To find an interesting newsgroup to read or
participate in, you might try one of these sites:

Who: USENET INFO CENTER LAUNCH PAD
Where: *http://sunsite.unc.edu/usenet-i/home
        .html*
What: Looking for a newsgroup to discuss gerbil
        raising or Tom Cruise? Try here, the
        Usenet Info Center, a complete
        information source on Usenet and its
        newsgroups. You can get help with Usenet
        commands, search for a group, browse
        Usenet groups, and find other Usenet
        indexes, such as DejaNews.

Who: DEJANEWS
Where: *http://www.dejanews.com/dnwhy.html*
What: Like the Usenet Info Center, DejaNews, the older and more established newsgroup resource, will help you find a group on the topic of your choice. It could be any subject, from artichoke soup recipes to tips on installing a Web server.

FINDING FRIENDS

There are several Web sites that are devoted just to finding people:

Who: BIGFOOT
Where: *http://www.bigfoot.com*
What: Bigfoot is an e-mail address finder. It also offers the opportunity for keeping the same e-mail address for life.

Who: WHO? WHERE?
Where: *http://whowhere.com*
What: This is probably the most popular white pages service on the Internet, and it includes an excellent index of personal Web pages.

FINDING IT IN THE LIBRARY

There are plenty of libraries that have their Web sites on the Internet available for you to access:

Who: LIBRARY OF CONGRESS
Where: *http://www.loc.gov*
What: Here's the granddaddy of all libraries. It's

the ultimate database for doing your history research—or any kind of research. Included is the "American Memory" site, a changing special collection dedicated to honoring the past. The current exhibit has a lot of interesting facts and pictures about the famous magician Harry Houdini.

Who: THE INTERNET PUBLIC LIBRARY
Where: *http://ipl.sils.umich.edu/*
What: The IPL Online Texts Collection, newly revised, now offers full searching and browsing by author, title, and Dewey decimal system subject on over 3,700 items. Read a new story in the Youth Division, such as "It's Magic!" Need help coming up with a science fair project? Check out the Science Fair Project Resource Guide, featuring Dr. Internet. There's a "Cars & Stuff" section, featuring "So You Want to Make a Car" and "Cars & History." Another great section is "Ask the Author," where children's book authors and illustrators answer your questions.

Who: AMAZON BOOKS
Where: *http://www.amazon.com*
What: This is "the world's largest online bookstore," and while it's not exactly a library, this is a good place to look for that book you need for your homework assignment—or for just a fun read. You can order books from them with a credit card and your parents' permission!

Who: ENCYCLOPEDIA BRITANNICA
ONLINE
Where: *http://www.eb.com/*
What: Britannica Online is a virtual
encyclopedia online. It's a commercial
service, which means you'll have to
subscribe to be able to access the more
than 14 million word hypertext database.
But there is a demo area where you can
get a taste of what it's like, and whether
it's for you.

FINDING OUT ABOUT THE WEATHER

Who: THE WEATHER CHANNEL
Where: *http://www.weather.com*
What: Everyone talks about the weather. At this
site, you can find out what the weather is
anywhere in the world.

Who: THE INTERNET WEATHER REPORT
Where: *http://www.internetweather.com/*
What: For a different kind of weather—what it's
like out there on the Web—check out this
site that tracks traffic on the Internet. The
report bounces packets to various IP
addresses, then measures how corrupt the
information is when it comes back. The
more corrupt, the more traffic in that area.
The information is updated every fifteen
minutes.

CYBERSARGE SAYS:

If the Internet Weather Report gives your Internet service provider a red flag, don't worry too much. Like everwhere else, traffic on the Internet is worse on some days than others.

FINDING SOFTWARE

More and more software is now available for downloading right off the Internet.

Who: TUCOWS
Where: ***http://www.tucows.com***
What: This site is your best Web source for shareware and freeware software. If what you want isn't here, you probably don't want it. You can even request a weekly e-mail update of what's new.

FINDING COMPUTER HELP

Most computer manufacturers and software companies have online Web sites, and these sites can be great sources of help when you've got a glitch in your machine.

Who: IBM
Where: ***http://www.ibm.com***
What: This is the home page for all IBM products, from software to hardware. Links from here get you to online ordering, IBM news, technical support, and articles about computing.

Who: APPLE COMPUTER WEB SITE
Where: ***http://www.apple.com/***
What: Get online technical support for Apple products, answers to questions, and software updates. Find out all about Apple's plans for future versions of the Macintosh operating system. Learn what

happened at the MacWorld Expo, or hear
RealAudio broadcasts of different
MacWorld magazine speakers.

Who: MICROSOFT ONLINE
Where: *http://www.microsoft.com*
What: If it's Windows related, then it must be
here. Everything Microsoft, including the
latest version of their Internet Explorer, is
here. Microsoft Online includes a lot of
helpful tips and tricks.

4. LEARNING

Explore inner as well as outer space at these sites.
Learn about the latest scientific discoveries, and get
ideas for that science fair project.

LEARNING ABOUT SCIENCE

Who: DISCOVERY CHANNEL ONLINE
Where: *http://www.discovery.com/*
What: Science, technology, exploration, history,
and nature all are here at your fingertips.
Nearly every week the Galileo spacecraft
beams back amazing information and
images from its voyage around Jupiter and
the planet's largest moons. NASA and
Discovery Online welcome you to chat
directly with the scientist-engineers
behind this exciting project. Come armed
with questions and curiosity!

Who: THE HUBBLE SPACE TELESCOPE'S
GREATEST HITS

Where: *http://www.stsci.edu/pubinfo/BestOfHST 95.html*

What: See a storm on Saturn big enough to swallow the Earth! See the Shoemaker-Levy Comet strike Jupiter! See a black hole! See all this and more by looking at some great photos at this site!

Who: THE NASA HOME PAGE

Where: *http://shuttle.nasa.gov*

What: This site is busiest during shuttle flights, and contains info on the crew, what the shuttle's mission is (unless it's classified!), and space activities. You can download shuttle pictures and sound bites, and watch the same map of the world that the NASA folks at Houston's mission control are watching.

Who: NEUROSCIENCE FOR KIDS

Where: *http://weber.u.washington.edu/~chudler /neurok.html*

What: With plenty of experiments, activities, and games, this site is for elementary and secondary school students and teachers who would like to learn more about the nervous system. Want to know how the brain is connected to the spinal cord, or how the senses work? Well, this is the place to find out.

Who: LAKE AFTON PUBLIC OBSERVATORY
Where: *http://www.uc.twsu.edu:80/~obswww/*
What: A part of the Fairmount Center for Science and Mathematics Education at Wichita State University, this Kansas site is yet another Web destination bringing outer space to cyberspace. One nice feature is "Ask an Astronomer" where you can get answers to those tough questions such as "Why is the sky blue?"

Who: NANOTECHNOLOGY
Where: *http://nano.xerox.com/nano*
What: Looking for something really, really small? Well, you've come to the right site. Here you'll find everything you want to know about the science of nanotechnology.

Who: KIDS' SPACE CONNECTION
Where: *http://www.KS-connection.com/*
What: The Kids' Space Connection is a great gathering place on the Net. It has creative activities, communication pages, and sections to help you learn basic computer skills. This site is really popular and has a worldwide following of Internauts from more than 115 countries.

Who: THE EXPLORATORIUM
Where: *http://www.exploratorium.edu/*
What: Explora Net is the World Wide Web site for the Exploratorium, the fun San Francisco museum of science, art, and human perception. The museum has over

650 interactive hands-on exhibits, some of which you can visit online. It also has a really cool digital library.

Who: STUDENTS FOR THE EXPLORATION & DEVELOPMENT OF SPACE
Where: *http://www.seds.org/*
What: The Lunar and Planetary Laboratory SEDS is a student-based organization about space exploration. It includes lots of great space photos, links to NASA and other sites, and the latest news about what's going on in outer space.

Who: STARCHILD: A LEARNING CENTER FOR YOUNG ASTRONOMERS
Where: *http://heasarc.gsfc.nasa.gov/docs/ StarChild/StarChild.html*
What: The StarChild Web site has a lot of information for younger and older kids about the solar system, stars, and planets. You'll need QuickTime or an AVI movie player to run the videos.

LEARNING ABOUT READING AND WRITING

Who: THE CHILDREN'S LITERATURE HOME PAGE
Where: *http://www.ucalgary.ca/~dkbrown/index. html*
What: This site is a great guide to children's literature on the Internet. It has lists of award-winning books and recommended reading, and includes suggestions from

the American Library Association.
Gopher links lead to information about
kids' authors, electronic children's books,
and other resources. This is a great place
to do research for that book report!

LEARNING ABOUT MONEY

Who: THE YOUNG INVESTOR
Where: *http://www.younginvestor.com/*
What: The Young Investor teaches kids the
basics of investing with articles on
everything from taxes to portfolios to
money. There's an investment game room
and The Measure Up Survey, a contest for
kids to win prizes based on their
understanding of money matters.

Who: MICROSOFT INVESTOR
Where: *http://www.investor.msn.com*
What: This is a free service of Microsoft
Network that has lots of information on
stocks, bonds, and investment strategies.

LEARNING ABOUT OUR WORLD

Who: ODYSSEY IN EGYPT
Where: *http://www.scriptorium.org/news/
articles/24hours_2.3.97.html*
What: Believe it or not, you can participate in an
online archaeological project in Egypt!
Visit this Web site to learn about last
year's discoveries and how you can get
involved in this year's projects.

Who: MAP QUEST
Where: *http://www.mapquest.com*
What: Map Quest is a fun place to visit and a great reference resource. Pick any location in the world, and a map of that area will pop up on your screen. You can get directions between any two places in the United States. One of the fun and useful things you can do on this site is create a street map that highlights where you live, which you can print out or attach to your e-mail messages.

Who: NATIONAL GEOGRAPHIC
Where: *http://www.nationalgeographic.com*
What: If you like to thumb through *National Geographic* magazines, you'll love turning these Web pages. There's a brand new issue every month, and a section just for kids.

Who: LONELY PLANET
Where: *http://www.lonelyplanet.com*
What: Lonely Planet offers travel guides to exotic and faraway places, like Ambon, Kashgar, and Timbuktu. This site also provides travel tips and even health advice. (Main tip when traveling: Get all your shots before you go!) Explore all those faraway places you've heard about, and discover some new places.

LEARNING ABOUT NATURE

Who: VIRTUAL GARDEN
Where: *http://pathfinder.com/@@EucPNeG6g
AAAQISI/vg/*
What: There is a really amazing plant
encyclopedia contained in this fascinating
online garden. Even if you don't have a
green thumb, you should enjoy digging
around in here.

Who: BROOKLYN BOTANIC GARDEN
Where: *http://www.bbg.org*
What: Just a short subway trip from Manhattan,
this is a virtual garden that is fun to
explore, and a useful botanical reference
resource.

Who: THE RAPTOR CENTER
Where: *http://www.raptor.cvm.umn.edu/*
What: No, it's not another dinosaur domain. The
raptors here are birds of prey, like owls,
eagles, and hawks. There are cool sights
and sounds, and you'll learn how the
Center is working to preserve and protect
these birds.

Who: BEES IN THE WEB
Where: *http://gears.tucson.ars.ag.gov/*
What: This hive of activity tells you everything
you want to know about bees. Read about
interesting bee facts in the "Internet
Classroom" and "Tribeeal Pursuits," and
learn what to do if you meet an angry
swarm of Africanized honey bees. Their
sensible advice: Run!

Who: MUSEUM OF PALEONTOLOGY

Where: *http://www.ucmp.berkeley.edu/*

What: Go to this site for a full-featured online tour of the Museum of Paleontology at the University of California, Berkeley. Like dinosaurs? You'll love this cybertour of the famous dinosaur collection at the University of California in Berkeley.

LEARNING ABOUT HISTORY

Who: THE '80S

Where: *http://www.80s.com*

What: Return to those thrilling days of the 1980s! This site is "like totally rad" because you can play '80s trivia, hear songs from the '80s, and read interesting articles about the whole decade.

Who: THE 1893 CHICAGO WORLD'S FAIR

Where: *http://xroads.virginia.edu/~MA96/WCE/title.html*

What: This site focuses on what the World's Columbian Exposition looked like, who was there, and what was on display. Don't miss the virtual tour of the fairgrounds, and see what it was like to be entertained at the turn of the century.

Who: DUKE PAPYRUS ARCHIVE

Where: *http://scriptorium.lib.duke.edu/papyrus/texts/homepage.html*

What: Egyptian papyri—over 1,300 of them—are cataloged here, with descriptions, translations, and images of the documents. It's really amazing to see how scholars have recreated an entire ancient world from these scraps of linen paper.

Who: THE VIKING NETWORK
Where: *http://odin.nls.no/viking/vnethome.htm*
What: This Norwegian Web site is the place to find out about the Vikings (no, not the football team!) and their life and times.

Who: CANADIAN MUSEUM OF CIVILIZATION
Where: *http://www.cmcc.muse.digital.ca/cmc/ cmceng/exhibeng.html*
What: Welcome to the Canadian Museum of Civilization. Here's a place where you can learn all about the history of our neighbor to the north, Canada.

Who: MUSEUM OF PHOTOGRAPHY
Where: *http://cmp1.ucr.edu*
What: The University of California at Riverside has an interesting online Museum of Photography. This site includes things such as news and historical photographs, and a collection of turn-of-the-century glass plate and stereoscopic images.

LEARNING WHAT'S NEW IN THE NEWS

Who: THE ELECTRONIC TELEGRAPH
Where: *http://www.telegraph.co.uk*
What: Great Britain's first electronic newspaper, *The Electronic Telegraph*, contains news

CYBERSARGE SAYS:

Several sites want you to register and enter a special password. Keeping track of these can be a headache. One tip is to use a program such as Windows Notepad to create a text file (name this file "Password"). When you forget the password required to log on to a site, you can open this notepad file and find out what it is.

PIN

PIN stands for Personal Identification Number and is used for cards for automated bank machines to make sure the person using the card owns the card. They are personal passwords that allow you to use the card to withdraw money or perform other services.

of the world that we sometimes can't find in the United States. When you register with the *Electronic Telegraph* to receive your news online, you will receive a **PIN** number, which you'll have to remember. As with all passwords and numbers, write your PIN down somewhere and don't tell anyone what it is.

Who: SAN JOSE MERCURY
Where: *http://www.sjmercury.com*
What: The online edition of the *San Jose Mercury* is located in northern California's Silicon Valley, which is the home of many major computer hardware and software companies, including Hewlett-Packard and Apple Computer.

Who: TIME
Where: *http://pathfinder.com/@@6jj7XwYAWZZ PUTm3/time/*
What: *Time Magazine* has a jam-packed World Wide Web page with photos and articles from their current issues and back-issue archives.

Who: TIMECAST
Where: *http://www.timecast.com*
What: Timecast is a RealAudio clearing house, kind of an online radio station where you can switch stations and listen to live sports broadcasts, news, commentaries, and music in all formats.

Who: MSNBC
Where: *http://www.msnbc.com/news/*
What: Microsoft teams up with NBC to provide
        news, sports, weather, and other
        interesting stuff. This magazine has a
        jam-packed World Wide Web page.

5. PLAYING

Want to have fun? Whether it's online games,
hobbies, or following your favorite sports team, here
are some great places to start:

FUN PLACES TO VISIT

Who: CALVIN & HOBBES
Where: *http://www.uexpress.com/cgi-bin/ups/*
        mainindex.cgi?code=ch
What: Meet Calvin & Hobbes, the famous boy
        and his tiger pal, and their creator, Bill
        Watterson.

Who: YOUR RULE SCHOOL
Where: *http://www.youruleschool.com/*
What: This Web site is sponsored by General
        Mills. First thing you have to do is sign up
        for a locker and get your very own secret
        combination. Once you get your locker,
        check out the Home Room, where you'll
        meet other classmates. Check out the
        Grub Club for inside information on free
        General Mills stuff. In the Yumnasium
        you'll get to play with your food and the
        Laugheteria serves up interactive fun
        twenty-four hours a day.

CYBERSARGE SAYS:

*There are
lots of
online news-
papers and
magazines
from all over the world. Some
of them have excellent databases of information. Do a
search to locate a newspaper
in your particular city, or try
reading a foreign newspaper!*

Who: THROUGH THE LINKING GLASS
Where: *http://www.kidsweb.org/*
What: Here's a fun page that leads visitors through several World Wide Web scavenger hunt games. It also has postcards you can e-mail to your friends showing them how you did on the hunts.

Who: SCHOLASTIC ONLINE
Where: *http://scholastic.com/*
What: Although this is a subscription service (you must pay a fee), there are free places to visit, including "Goosebumps," "The Magic Schoolbus," and "The Babysitters' Club."

Who: CYBERTOWN
Where: *http://www.cybertown.com/3dvd.html*
What: Cybertown is a virtual reality site, with links to other VR sites. You can inhabit and travel these worlds using avatars, which are digital representations of yourself. Some of the worlds have music and other sounds, and if you're using CoolTalk (available as a Netscape plug-in), you can talk to other avatars.

Who: LEGO
Where: *http://www.lego.com/*
What: If you are one of the millions who love LEGO products and want to know all about them, you're in the right place.

Who: THE BEATLES PAGE
Where: *http://www.primenet.com/~dhaber/ beatles.html*
What: Here you'll find tons of Fab Four info and trivia—more than you could ever imagine, including links for ordering rare Beatles outtakes and CDs. You can also subscribe to a Beatles newsgroup.

IF YOU'RE INTO SPORTS

Who: SPORTSLINE
Where: *http://cbs.sportsline.com*
What: Scores, stats, videos, superstar athletes, and the Web's Internet-only sports radio station can all be found here.

Who: ESPNET SPORTZONE
Where: *http://www.sportszone.com*
What: This site is for sports fans of all ages. It provides constantly updated scores, stats, and game recaps. It also has information on upcoming games, including World Cup soccer. You can also download pictures of your favorite players and look at them whenever you want!

Who: TOTAL BASEBALL ONLINE
Where: *http://www.totalbaseball.com/*
What: Total Baseball Online is the online home of the Official Encyclopedia of Major League Baseball. This site celebrates the game's glorious past with biographies, team histories, statistical summaries, and baseball chat.

Who: SPORTS ILLUSTRATED FOR KIDS

Where: *http://pathfinder.com/@@g*7nZgQA720 Th*S1/SIFK/*

What: This is an online, interactive version of *Sports Illustrated* that's just for kids. You can send in questions, find out which sports heroes share your birthday, and play some exciting interactive games.

PUZZLES AND OTHER DISTRACTIONS

Who: THE CASE

Where: *http://www.thecase.com/*

What: Write your own mystery! If the folks at the Case select it, it will get printed on their Web page. The Case is the premiere mystery Web site on the Internet. It provides three high-quality mysteries weekly, including a "Twist" surprise ending, a "Solve-It" mini-mystery, and a "Mysterious Photo" mystery. The "Solve-It" and "Mysterious Photo" mysteries both include weekly contests with prizes. Let's see how smart you really are!

ENTERTAINMENT

Who: NICK AT NIGHT'S TV LAND

Where: *http://nickatnitestvland.com/*

What: This site has a huge collection of clips, sounds, and video from TV Land programming. Play the fun quizzes on the old TV shows airing on Nick at Night. You'll need a Java browser to hear the sound clips, including "da-da-da-daah, snap-snap" from "The Addams Family."

Who: X-FILES
Where: *http://www.rutgers.edu/x-files.html*
What: This is the home page of the popular TV show "The X-Files." This site has links to lots of X-Files FAQs and other sites. Play the theme music, listen to the promo for the fall season, scan the episode guide, and read what X-Files fans have to say about the episodes.

Who: FOX INTERACTIVE
Where: *http://www.foxinteractive.com/*
What: Discover all the action of Fox Interactive's current titles, or go behind the scenes to find out about upcoming releases. You can also get technical help in Tech Support, dive into reviews and press releases, and explore some of the secrets you'll encounter playing these games.

Who: THE OFFICIAL STAR WARS WEB SITE
Where: *http://www.starwars.com/*
What: To advertise the re-release of the legendary *Star Wars* trilogy, LucasFilms created this exciting site. Full of images, games, and updates, these pages are bound to appeal to fans of the movie series, which first opened in 1977. You'll need Shockwave and a sound player plug-in to play some of the games.

Who: ANIMANIACS
Where: *http://www2.msstate.edu/~jbp3/animx/*
       animx.html
What: This is the "Animaniacs" home page. Not
       quite as neat as "The X-Files" page, but it
       has the "alt.tv.animaniacs New Reader's
       Guide," a must-read "Quick Start" list of
       services and references available.

Who: THE SITE
Where: *http://www.thesite.com/*
What: Here is the online version of MSNBC's
       TV show dealing with trends in
       computers and cyberspace. Most recently
       on The Site was the text of a televised
       interview with William Gibson, author of
       the novel *Neuromancer* (where he coined
       the word "cyberpunk.") The Site also has
       a TV program airing nightly on the new
       MSNBC cable channel.

Who: PARAMOUNT PICTURES
Where: *http://paramount.com*
What: This is the home page of Paramount
       Pictures with information on their TV
       shows and movies, including a "Star Trek:
       Voyager" home page.

Who: SONY
Where: *http://www.music.sony.com*
What: This is where you can find all sorts of
       information on Sony recording artists,
       their concerts, music, video clips, and
       much more.

GAMES

Who: SEGA
Where: *http://www.sega.com*
What: Sega, the game manufacturer, has its own Web site. Here you can find the latest updates on their catalog, price lists, and demos of their latest games to download.

Who: EXSCAPE FROM REALITY
Where: *http://www.exscape.com/*
What: Exscape is a Web site for gamers, with demos of popular games, shareware, tips, and cool graphics. This site is the creation of two teenage cousins. Their reviews are hip, but be prepared to wait while the pages load.

Who: HAPPY PUPPY GAME SITE
Where: *http://happypuppy.com*
What: If you're into video games, then this place was made for you. Happy Puppy has games and also lots of reviews, hints, and walk-throughs of other popular games.

Who: NINTENDO
Where: *http://www.nintendo.com/*
What: Nintendo's Web site has links to Acclaim, maker of Turok, Dinosaur Hunter, and to other game pages. There's not much for kids to do unless you like reading about Nintendo's marketing strategy, or seeing new advertising for their games.

Who: WORLD CONQUEST
Where: *http://www.dnai.com/~conquest*
What: This is the site of an online multiplayer strategy game called World Conquest.

REVIEW YOUR FAVORITE SITES

If you have comments on any of CyberSarge's favorites, or if you find some of your own, you can make copies of this form to write down your thoughts:

WHO?: The name of the Web site.
WHERE?: The URL address.
WHAT?: What's it all about?
WHY?: Why do I like this site?

You can e-mail your comments and reviews to CyberSarge at *kids@internet4kids.com*.

WHO? _____

WHERE? _____

_____

WHAT? _____

_____

_____

WHY? _____

_____

_____

_____

_____

_____

Chapter 8

Tech Talk:

Getting Online

Back in Chapter 2, Kate and Zack went through all the necessary steps for getting them online. But we didn't show you all the details of how they connected to the Internet. To make it easier for you, we decided to put all the specific steps right here in one chapter.

Different computers need different software programs to connect to the Internet. We will go through step-by-step instructions for installing the right programs for Windows 95, Windows 3.1, and Macintosh. Remember that the setup may be confusing at times, and you may want your parents to help you with this part. You can also call your ISP or online service to walk you through the steps. They are really helpful and knowledgeable!

When you sign up with an ISP, you'll probably get the basic software you need: a program to get your computer speaking the same language as Internet computers, a World Wide Web browser, and mail and newsreader programs. All of these programs will be on floppy disks or a CD-ROM, so that the information can be transferred to your computer's hard drive. These disks contain information that will connect your computer to the Internet. They're the energy source for your trip into cyberspace!

Kate's and Zack's computer is running Windows 95, so we'll start with that. Those of you with different operating systems can skip ahead to the one you're using.

WINDOWS 95

Dial-Up Networking

First of all, make sure you have *Dial-Up Networking* installed on your computer. If your computer came with Windows 95 already installed, you most likely do. If you don't have Dial-Up Networking, you will need to install it with the Windows 95 installation disk. Double-click on *My Computer* and a window will open up showing the disk drives you have: a folder icon for *Printers*, one for *Control Panel* and one for *Dial-Up Networking*. If the Dial-Up Networking folder is there, jump ahead to *Getting Connected*. If it isn't, just follow along:

1. Open *Control* and click on *Add/Remove Programs*.

2. In the *Add/Remove Programs* window, select *Windows Setup*.

3. Pick the *Communications* option and select *Details*.

4. Select the *Dial-Up Networking* option. If prompted, insert the requested Windows installation disk or the CD-ROM.

5. Click on *OK* in the *Communications* box; click on *OK* in the *Add/Remove Programs* box.

Now you need to set up TCP/IP, the language you need for your computer to talk to Internet computers.

1. From the *Start* menu, pick *Settings*, then

Control Panel. Double-click the *Network* icon. Click the *Add* button, select *Protocol*, then the *Add* button again. The *Select Network Protocol* dialog box will appear. Select *Microsoft* from the Manufacturers' list, select *TCP/IP* from the *Network Protocols* list, then click on *OK*.

2. Now make sure the *Dial-Up Adapter* is using TCP/IP. In the *Network Dialog* box, select the *Dial-Up Adapter* to highlight it, click on the *Properties* button, then select the *Bindings* tab. There should be a check mark in the box next to the word *TCP/IP*. If there isn't, click on the check box to insert one.

3. Go back to the *Network* icon in the *Control Panel* box. Highlight *Dial-Up Adapter*, then select *Properties*. Select the *IP Address* tab and make sure the *Obtain IP Address Automatically* option is checked (unless your service provider gives you one, in which case you'll type it in).

4. In the *TCP/IP Properties* folder, click on the *DNS Configuration* tab. Select *Enable DNS*. Then enter the *Host name* (leave it blank or type in your name) and the *Domain name*—your provider's name, such as **mynet.com**. In the *DNS Server Search Order* box, enter the numbers your provider gave you. This will look something like: 198.200.20.1 (your numbers will vary).

5. Click *OK* to close *Network*. You'll have to exit Windows and restart the computer for the changes to take effect.

Getting Connected

Here's where you tell Windows 95 about the connection you're making to your ISP.

1. Open *My Computer* and double-click on the *Dial-Up Networking* icon. A *Connection Wizard* will start up to prompt you through the steps you need to take.

2. Enter the name of your service provider such as **mynet.com**

3. If you haven't set up your modem to work with Windows 95, here's where you do it. Click on *Configure* (follow your modem manufacturer's instructions).

4. Now click on *Next*. Here you'll enter the area code and phone number of your provider. Click on *Next*, then click *Finish* to complete the installation. You can drag the service provider's icon to your desktop for quicker access.

Setting Up For Your Provider

If you had to install Dial-Up Networking (see above), then some of these steps will already have been completed.

1. Click on your *New Connection* icon in the *My Computer* folder (or on your desktop if you've dragged the icon there). Click your *New Connection* and choose *Properties*. Choose *Server Type*.

2. Uncheck the boxes for *Software Compression*, *NetBEUI*, and *IPX/SPX*. Click *TCP/IP Settings*. Choose *Server Assigned IP Address* and *Specify Name Server Addresses*. Your service provider will have given you the numbers to enter for a primary DNS (see step 4 in *Getting Connected*). You might also enter a secondary DNS if you have one. Uncheck *Use IP Header Compression*. Hit *OK* until all windows are closed.

Finishing Up

Now just double-click on the icon for the connection you've just created, type in your user ID and password, and you'll be connected!

WINDOWS 3.1

Connecting to the Internet using Windows 3.1 is a bit harder than with Windows 95 because Windows 3.1 doesn't automatically install and recognize modems and Internet software. You'll need to do two things: Set up your computer to talk to Internet computers (by installing TCP/IP), and set up your modem to talk to your service provider.

Here are the basic steps:

1. Install the Internet dialer software you got from your ISP, following the instructions (we can't tell you how since there are so many different software packages available). The installation will create a new menu called *Program Group*, which will probably contain the name of your ISP or the software package it uses. This new *Program Group* will contain icons for your Internet dialer software.

2. Set up the dialer program with your provider's IP address.

3. Type in your computer's name (the *Host*) and your provider's computer's name (the *Domain*.)

4. Set up the dialer software to recognize your modem, including the *Port* (usually Com 1 or Com 2), the **baud rate**, and any other information the software requires.

5. Now set up the software to dial up your provider. Type in the phone number your

BAUD RATE

Baud rate refers to the speed at which a modem sends data over telephone lines, as measured in bits per second. For example, your modem speed may be 14.4, 28.8, or 33.3. You will need to know this information in order to get online.

provider gave you, and the log-in name and password you've arranged.

6. If your provider gave you numbers for *Default Gateway* and *Domain Servers*, you'll need to type them in the appropriate boxes as well.

7. Your provider will possibly have other servers for mail and news, two important Internet services. Enter those numbers to finish the dialer set up. Then just open the *Program Group* and click on the *dialer* to connect.

MACINTOSH

Macs are the easiest computers to set up for the Internet. A lot of the work is done for you, and Apple provides the software to connect to your provider.

In most cases, your Internet provider will supply you with software that automatically configures your Mac for an Internet connection. If so, you should consult the software manuals or installation instructions that your provider gives you. If your provider's software automatically configures your Mac for the Internet, then you don't need to read the rest of this section.

If your Internet provider doesn't supply software to configure your Mac automatically, you will need to enter certain information yourself. To do this, be sure that you have the following information: your provider's *gateway address* number, its *domain name*, and its *IP address*. You may also need a name server address number. Your Internet provider will be able to supply you with all of these.

Depending on the type of Mac you have and the version of Mac System Software it uses, there are several different files you should be sure are installed on your Mac for successful Internet connection. If these files are not present on your system, consult the user guides and software installation instructions that came with your Mac for information on how to install them:

1. **MacTCP or TCP/IP**. These are two versions of software that make it possible for your Mac to talk to other computers over the Internet. One or the other of these files, but not both, should be in the *Control Panels* folder in your Mac's *System Folder*.

2. **PPP, MacPPP, and FreePPP**. These files help your Mac communicate with your Internet provider. One or all of these files should be in the *Extensions* folder in your Mac's *System Folder*.

3. **Dialer Software**. There are many different kinds of "dialers" that help your Mac connect to your Internet provider through your modem. The most commonly used one is ConfigPPP, which may be included in your Internet provider's software, or with the Internet software that comes with your Mac. Consult the guides or installation instructions that come with your software to see how to configure the dialer you have.

There are two ways to make an Internet configuration on your Mac. If you have the control panel called MacTCP, follow steps one through five. If you have the control panel called TCP/IP, follow steps six through eight.

1. Open *MacTCP* in *Control Panels*. You should see an icon for *FreePPP* or one of the other PPP files mentioned above. Choose one. Click on *More. . .* at the bottom.

2. Click on *Manually* in the top left-hand corner.

Go down to the lower left and type in the *Gateway Address*. Now go to the top right and change the *Class* to *C*.

3. Go down to the lower right and insert the *Domain Name* and the *IP Address*.

4. Go back to the top left-hand corner and check *Server*. Click *OK* or *Done*.

5. Close *MacTCP* window. You should get a warning box telling you to restart in order for the changes to take place. Click *OK* on the message and restart the computer.

If you have the Control Panel called **TCP/IP**, follow these steps:

6. Open *TCP/IP* in *Control Panels*. Use the first pull-down menu, *Connect Via*, to select either *FreePPP* or *MacPPP*. Use the second pull-down menu, *Configure Using*, to select *PPP Server*. The *IP address*, *Subnet Mask*, and *Router Address* will now say: *will be provided by server*. This means that the information for those items will be sent by your Internet provider when you make a connection. You do not have to enter information into those places yourself.

7. Enter the *Name Server Address*, which will be a group of four (or less) three-digit numbers separated by periods. Enter the *Starting Domain Name*, the *Ending Domain Name*, or the *Search Domains* only if they have been supplied to you by your Internet provider.

8. Click on *Done* or *OK*. Save the changes and close TCP/IP. Now you're ready to dial your provider.

USING A COMMERCIAL SERVICE

If you use America Online, CompuServe, or Microsoft Network, not only will you avoid going through all the configuration steps above, but you most likely won't need any more software once you're online. The commercial services offer many different options. You can check the news or weather, read sports scores, or chat with other people. But if you're using a service provider, you'll need more software programs to do something once you've connected your computer to your ISP. We've talked about mail and newsreaders, chat software, and Web browsers earlier in the book. Here's where you learn how to get them up and running on the Internet.

SETTING UP YOUR WEB BROWSER

As we've said, you'll probably want to use either Netscape Navigator or Microsoft Internet Explorer as your World Wide Web browser. Whichever one you decide on, both will provide tools to send and receive mail and news, as well as the ability to cruise the Web.

Chances are you received Explorer or Navigator as part of the software package from your ISP, on floppy disks or a CD-ROM. To install your browser, put the disk in the drive and follow the instructions from your provider. Most likely, you'll type *Setup* or *Install*, and the program will do the rest of the work.

Both Explorer and Navigator offer Internet mail and Internet newsgroup readers, so if you don't want to install and learn another program, this is the way to go. Let's start with Netscape.

NETSCAPE MAIL SETUP

Here's how to configure Netscape Navigator for e-mail:

1. Start Netscape by double-clicking on the icon you've dragged to your desktop or the file located in the C: drive. (If your computer starts to dial up your server, hit the *Stop* button).

2. Click on the *Options* menu. Select *Mail and News Preferences*. Ignore the *Appearance* and *Composition* tabs.

3. You will see five menu options. Start with *Servers*. Fill in the name your provider gives you for incoming and outgoing mail server names. They might be *SMTP* and *POP*, or *mail*. For example, your SMTP server might be named **smtp.mynet.com**; your mail server **mail.mynet.com**. Set *Check for Mail Every ___ Minutes* to *Never* if you want to disable the automatic checking of new mail.

4. Go to *Identity*. Fill in your name (remember, not your full name), and your *Outgoing* and *Reply To* e-mail address (for example, **kate@mynet.com**). If you want, you can create a *signature file* that Netscape will attach to every e-mail message you send.

5. Select the *Organization* tab. Check the box marked *Remember Mail Password*. The first time you use Netscape mail to access your provider's mail server, it'll ask you for your password (which should be the same as your log-in password). After that, you won't be prompted again.

SIGNATURE FILE

A signature file is a small plain text (ASCII) file you create in your word processor. It will be attached to every e-mail that you send.

It can be plain:

Sincerely, ZACK

or fancy:

Be the best you can be.

Zack.

You can e-mail me at zack@mynet.com

NETSCAPE NEWS SETUP

1. Just as with Mail, start Netscape, click on the *Options* menu, and then *Mail and News Preferences*.

2. Type the name of your News (NNTP) server. (Mine is "news.")

3. Netscape suggests creating a *News RC Directory*, which is a directory on your hard drive where Netscape will store all received items. But you can change it if you want.

4. Type in the number of articles to be viewed at a time (3500 maximum).

INTERNET EXPLORER MAIL SETUP

1. Open Microsoft's Internet Explorer. Click on *Mail*. The first time you open the mail applet, the configuration menu opens automatically. If it doesn't, click on *Read Mail*, then *Options*.

2. Just as with Netscape's mail program, you need to provide the name of your SMTP and POP3 servers. Select the *Server* tab and fill in your *name*, *e-mail address* (for example, **kate@mynet.com**), *Incoming and Outgoing mail servers*, your *POP3 Account* (your e-mail address to the left of the "@" sign), and your *password*.

INTERNET EXPLORER NEWS SETUP

1. Open Microsoft's Internet Explorer. Click on *Mail*. If this is the first time you're here, the Setup menu will open. Otherwise, select *Read News*, then *News* and then *Options*.

2. Select the *Server* tab. Again, just as with

Netscape's news program, Explorer requires the name of your *news server*, your *account name* and *password* on your news server. (Many news servers do not require a password. Ask your service provider whether you will need one.)

3. Fill in your *e-mail address*. This is the address that people should use when responding to a message that you post to a newsgroup.

OTHER NEWS AND MAIL PROGRAMS

Eudora (for Macs and PCs), WinVN (for PCs), and NewsWatcher (for Macs) are among the many stand-alone mail programs. Though their setup procedures will vary somewhat, they all require the same setup information.

PLUG-INS

In addition, you'll probably want to add some plug-ins to make the fullest use of the sights and sounds on the Web. Netscape automatically logs on to its home site at:

http://home.netscape.com

and takes you to a page where you can select which plug-ins you want. Microsoft's plug-in Web site is located at:

http://microsoft.com/msdownload/

That's it! Now you're a real pro, ready and able to help your friends dive into the fun and adventure on the Internet.

YOUR CHECKLIST OF ISP INFORMATION

Use the next page to write down the important information about your Internet service provider. Keep it in a safe place near your computer.

Name of ISP: _____

ISP Web address: _____

ISP technical support phone number: _____

Your log-on phone number: _____

Log-on user name: _____

Log-on user password: _____

E-mail server address: _____

Password: _____

News server address: _____

Password: _____

Your modem type and speed: _____

Your Web browser software: _____

Your e-mail software: _____

Your newsgroup software: _____

Notes: _____

_____

_____

_____

_____

_____

_____

_____

_____

USING YOUR WEB BROWSERS

Now that you're online, let's take a brief look at your Web browser and how to use the commands and buttons to get around online.

1. **FILE**: This menu allows you to treat a Web page just like any other document, printing, saving to your hard drive, and closing documents.

2. **EDIT**: Here you can cut and copy URLs or other text, or search a Web page for a word or phrase.

3. **VIEW**: This list of commands includes changing the look of your browser, reloading pages, or stopping a transfer.

4. **GO**: Go allows you to jump to other pages you've visited during the current session.

5. **BOOKMARKS**: (Explorer calls them *Favorites*.) Here you can save in a file the addresses of special sites you've been to so you can revisit them without having to type in an address all over again.

6. **HELP**: Click here to find an online help site.

These commands are exclusive to Netscape:

1. **OPTIONS**: You can change the way Netscape displays pages, set up mail and newsreaders, and view other features. (This choice appears under *View* in Explorer.)

2. **DIRECTORY**: This is where you can find several Netscape World Wide Web destinations.

3. **WINDOW**: This option lets you choose what is on the screen: *Mail, News, Bookmarks*, or *Address Book*.

Both Netscape and Explorer include buttons that duplicate some menu commands, such as *Back* to previous pages; *Forward*, available only after you've gone back; *Home* to whatever your default start page is; *Reload* the page, if transfer is interrupted; and *Stop* loading, if you get tired of waiting for a slow site to respond. All of these commands make it much simpler for you to surf the Web.

SENDING AND RECEIVING E-MAIL

If you've already set up your mail reader, you're ready to send and receive electronic mail. Here's how:

1. Dial up your service provider and get online.

2. Open your mail program.

3. If it's set up correctly, the program will automatically check for any mail you've received. In addition, you will often be alerted about waiting mail by an icon or voice alert. Unless your provider sends a welcome message to new subscribers, or you've told a friend or relative to send you mail, you won't have any.

4. Send yourself an e-mail letter. Type in a *Subject* ("Test") and some sample text ("This is a test"). Be sure to type in your *Address* correctly (for example, *zack@mynet.com*).

5. In a second or so, depending on how busy the Internet is, you should receive your mail. If your mail program is open, an *In* mailbox will pop up on your screen showing the sender—you!—the time received, the size, and other information. Or an icon or sound will let you know that you have mail waiting to be read.

6. Now you can begin collecting e-mail addresses

from your friends and relatives. Your e-mail program probably has an *Address Book* where you can enter those addresses. You can just click to select who you want to send your letter to from this list.

JOINING A NEWSGROUP

1. Log on.

2. Open your browser.

3. Visit the DejaNews or the Info Center Launch Pad sites (see *Chapter 7: Guide to the Galaxy, page 121* for the URL). You can search for newsgroup topics by name, just as you would when doing a World Wide Web search.

4. If you see a newsgroup topic that interests you, click on it and your browser will post a list of the most recent articles. You can read (and respond to) newsgroup articles in your browser.

5. If it seems like the kind of newsgroup you want to come back to, you can join (or subscribe). Here's how:

   A. Open your Netscape or Explorer Newsreader (unless you've installed another one, such as Free Agent or WinVN). Your ISP will ask you if you want to download the entire list of newsgroups. Click on *Yes*. This can be time- consuming, as there are over 20,000 newsgroups currently online.

   B. When the list appears, double-click on your chosen group to get a list of currently available articles. You'll see a sender's name and a topic. Most lists keep articles for about two weeks, then they are discarded. That's because disk space on list servers is limited, but the articles just keep on coming!

C.   Double-click on an article you want to read. Use your newsreader's controls to move through the articles. Don't forget to use the commands on the menu or the button **shortcuts** to respond to articles.

HOW TO DOWNLOAD A FILE

Lots of cool stuff on the Internet is kept in FTP sites. Utility programs, browser plug-ins, sound files, and games can be downloaded at the click of a mouse.

Most of the time, moving through an FTP site and downloading files will be pretty easy. These sites, when viewed through the friendly screen of your browser, will show their files as file folder icons and hypertext links. Clicking on a folder icon opens the directory it represents. Clicking on a link begins the download process.

HOW TO SAVE INFORMATION

When you want to save something that you've found on a Web page, you can save the text information as a file on your computer. Go to the *File* command on your browser and drag the mouse down to *Save As*. A window will open up and you will have the option of renaming this file or keeping the name of whatever that particular file is called. Just remember to note what directory the file is located in so you can find it easily. Also remember that usually you will be saving text only, not the graphics.

HOW TO CUSTOMIZE YOUR BROWSER

A really great thing about browsers is that you can customize your browser to log on to any site you

CYBERSARGE SAYS:

Be sure to download each file into its own directory on your hard drive! That way you'll know where to find it, and you can delete the useless files after you've completed the install process.

SHORTCUT

This is an icon on your desktop that represents a file or a Web site. Clicking on the shortcut will open the file or your Web browser, dial up your provider, and log you on to the site.

CYBERSARGE SAYS:

Create a text file (Zack and Kate use Windows Notepad). Call it "Cool Web Sites." Then, if someone tells you about a neat site you might want to visit, but you don't plan to go online any time soon, put the address and a short description in the file. Then when you do log on, you can cut the address from the file and paste it in the browser window to visit the site.

choose. You can start your online time there instead of starting at your provider's home page when you first log on. For instance, you can log directly on to your favorite game site or your favorite site that gives you the daily horoscope. Most ISPs have this option now, and there are lots of other ways to customize your browser. You can change the type that's displayed on the screen, the colors, and how the hypertext links appear. There are a few programs, like Microsoft Plus!, For Kids, or Surfwatch, that let you set a different start page for each member of your family.

1. In Netscape, open the *Options* menu, select *General Preferences*, then the *Appearance* tab. There you'll see a *Startup* box. Select *Browser Starts With*, and type in the URL address of the Web page where you want to begin your browser session.

2. In Explorer, select *View*, *Options*, and *Navigation*. There you can enter the name of the start page, search page and the various link pages you want.

INTERNET RELAY CHAT TECH NOTES

There's more to IRC than just typing out what's on your mind. IRC has its own special set of commands that allow you to join chat rooms and chat with the people you find there. Here are the most common IRC commands:

/list
This command lets you find out what IRC channels are available, their topics, and the number of users.

/join
Type this command, followed by the name of the

channel to join a channel. This is the same as */channel*, which is used on some IRCs.

/part

This is what you type to leave a channel, or you may type */leave*

/whois

This command will tell you more about the character you want to know about. Type */whois [nickname]* to see the contents of his or her profile.

/action /me /describe

These are action commands, which provide stage directions. For example, */action running and jumping* will put that action on everyone's screen in distinctive text, and */me crying* will indicate to everyone online that you're crying over what was just said.

/msg /notice /query

You can use */msg* and */notice* followed by the appropriate nickname to send private notes to a particular user so that everyone in the chat group doesn't see it. You can use */query [nickname]* to direct everything you type to that person so you don't have to keep typing in the nickname. It's like having a personal conversation in the middle of a crowded room.

/notify /ignore

While you're going to make friends online, there will also be people you'd rather not talk to. If

CYBERSARGE SAYS:

In Windows 95, you can drag a link from your browser and put it on your desktop as a shortcut.

you type */notify [nickname]*, you'll be notified when that particular person you want to avoid shows up. Typing */ignore [nickname]* will make sure you don't get any messages from that person.

PART III

Commander:
Welcome, Parents and Teachers

O:-) >:-) :-) =:-) :-o :-! :-' :-D :-* :-p (-8 :-"

KIDS! Have your parents read this!

In the following chapter, CyberSarge provides information for both parents and teachers about guiding adults in this fascinating adventure through the new world their kids have come to know as cyberspace. This chapter discusses issues that will help guide adults on this fascinating adventure throughout the Internet. Once the adult has read this information, he or she can use the Official Internet Contract on page 192, which both adult and child can amend, agree to, and then sign.

Chapter 9

Parents' Guide:

Where Are Your Kids Tonight on the Internet?

Sometimes parents can be more intimidated by the Internet than their kids. After all, you didn't grow up in a digital generation. But while cyberspace may seem strange and mysterious, it really isn't. The Internet is just a freeway system for computers. Instead of sitting alone in a room typing documents on a computer, you can experience a whole new universe of places to go, things to see, and people to visit on the Internet.

Your kids have been taken on a tour of the Internet with CyberSarge, a fictitious cartoon guy. They have been taught a lot, and if they've followed the book through to this point, they've even been promoted from Cadets to full-fledged Internauts. Now it's time for you to meet Cybersarge and read some notes

UNIVERSAL TRANSLATOR

specifically for parents and teachers. Of course, kids are welcome to read it, too. Since most Internet providers require that an adult sign up for the Internet service by pledging to pay monthly fees and other charges billed directly through a credit card, parents must be involved to a certain extent in their children's travels in cyberspace. Also, hooking up to the Internet involves using a modem. Unless you have a dedicated telephone line just for computer use, your phone line will be tied up whenever your kids are on the Internet. Having read through this book, your kids know that. And we have already covered many of these issues with your children, so we won't repeat them here. (See *Chapter 5: The Top Ten Rules for Surfing the Net, page 87.*)

However, CyberSarge believes that parents have a lot more at stake than just money and telephone time in their kids' involvement on the Internet. Assuming you parents and teachers are not already surfing the Net yourselves, your children will be introducing you to a new world with which many adults are only vaguely familiar. CyberSarge thinks that it would be a great idea for you to browse through this book as well. But if you don't have the time or the inclination, or even if you have already read this along with your kids, there are some issues that you should be aware of.

Your kids may be more conversant in "tech talk" than you are, but they need your experience and common sense to drive safely on the cyberspace freeways.

CYBERSARGE SAYS:

Right about now is the perfect time to take this book to your parents or teacher. Tell them to read **Chapter 9: Where Are Your Kids Tonight on the Internet? (page 183),** *which is a grown-ups' guide to helping their kids surf in cyberspace.*

| File | Edit | | View |

ISSUES FOR GROWN-UPS

Like our cities and neighborhoods, the Internet is okay most of the time. But there are still a few hidden dangers to be aware of.

Watching your kids venture out on the Internet is a bit like sending them off to school for the first time. Just as you teach your children to look both ways when crossing the street, and tell them not to accept rides from strangers, there are rules your children need to know when they are navigating the Net.

Your kids are entering a new and exciting place. And as parents and educators, you need to know what to look out for so you can advise them.

First of all, think of the Internet as a giant shopping mall. There are places in the mall that are okay for your kids to go into, and some places you've told them to stay away from. There are movies they can see, and movies they can't. There are rules, and as parents and teachers you've set up those rules and you expect your kids to follow them. When they don't, they're punished or "grounded." It should work the same way on the Internet. Being online is a privilege that you have given your children.

If your kids' connection to the Internet is through a commercial service like CompuServe or America Online, you should know that the administrators of these services take reasonable precautions to keep truly objectionable or offensive messages off their systems. But once on the

Internet, whether through a commercial service or an Internet service provider, there are no real barricades to keep children out of places they shouldn't be.

But that shouldn't frighten you. The real world is the same way. And the same rules apply on the Internet as in the real world.

Let's talk for a minute about the dangers on the Internet and the things you and your children can do to avoid them.

The first thing for you to remember is that the Internet is normally accessed through a phone line. When you answer the phone at home, if something or someone bothers you, you can just hang up. You can do the same thing on the Internet: Hang up, or go somewhere else.

The Internet is a "network of networks," meaning that there are millions of users all connected to one another through phone lines and computers in that vast unseeable place called cyberspace. One of the benefits of the Internet is that it is a forum where information is shared widely and freely and where educational material is literally at your fingertips. However, that freedom can also be a source of potential mischief. There is no one who is overseeing all the messages and files that are posted every second of the day.

Some newsgroups are moderated. That means there is a person in charge to keep the discussion on track and rein in "flamers," or people on the Net who enjoy picking fights or posting obscene messages. But many groups are not moderated. You can usually tell from the name of a list or newsgroup if it's something you want your kids to be reading. Fortunately, there are special forums set up for kids only that are monitored at all times. If you're not sure if a forum or newsgroup is moderated and/or appropriate for kids, you can send an e-mail letter to the forum sponsor and ask. You can also telephone or e-mail the online service you have chosen, and they will provide that information.

In addition, while the vast majority of folks on the Internet are okay, a very few may not be. There are people whose main purpose in life seems to be to go online and start fights. There are others who want to demean or belittle others, perhaps so they can feel superior. And a few seek to exploit or even harm others.

That's frightening, and it's easy to overreact—especially when you're facing new technology that your children may seem to understand better than you do. The outside world may have gotten more dangerous since you were a kid—but that's no reason to stay indoors. What is needed on the street is "street smarts." What you and your children need on the Internet is "cybersmarts." Be aware that:

1. Your child may be exposed to inappropriate material of a sexual or violent nature.

2. While online your child might provide personal information that could risk his or her safety, or the safety of other family members.

3. Your children might receive e-mail messages that are harassing, demeaning, or even sexually suggestive.

To help restrict your child's access to areas that contain inappropriate material, many of the commercial online services and some of Internet service providers have systems in place for parents to block out parts of the service they feel are inappropriate for their children. This is like locking out certain phone numbers or cable TV channels. If you are concerned, you should contact the service you're using or thinking of using, by telephone or e-mail, to find out how you can add these restrictions to any accounts that your children can access. There are also software programs that do this, and we'll talk about them at the end of this chapter.

The U.S. government is also in the process of evaluating obscenity and pornography use on the Internet. Cybercops, or Secret Service personnel who travel cyberspace, do prosecute some offenders. However, the Internet is a rather anarchical entity, changing every day. There is no way to keep up with all of the new information posted or to chase down every online flamer.

Therefore, the best way to assure that your children are having positive online experiences is to stay in touch with what they are doing. You can do this by spending time with your children while they're online. Have them show you what they do and ask them to teach you how to access the services they use.

Remember, the same general parenting skills that apply to the real world also apply while your kids are in cyberspace. While children need a certain amount of privacy, you know that they also need parental involvement and supervision in their daily lives. If you have cause for concern about your children's online activities, discuss it with them. By taking responsibility for your children's online computer use, you can greatly minimize any of the potential risks of being online.

Seek out the advice and counsel of other computer users in your area. Talk with your child's teacher or other parents and become familiar with the literature on the Internet. Open communication with your children is important. Also, if you use the same computer resources your children use and get online yourself, you will help obtain greater benefits. Who knows? You might even have as much fun and learn as much as they do! And being online yourself may alert you to potential problems that may occur there.

It's important that you educate yourself and become computer literate. Get to know your child's online friends just as you get to know all of their other friends.

Make it a firm rule that your children **never** give out identifying information—full name, home address, school name, or telephone number. If one of your child's Net pals lives nearby, they may want to meet face-to-face. Making friends online is great, but you should never allow your child to arrange a face-to-face meeting with another computer user you do not know. No matter how harmless it might seem, it is absolutely NOT a good idea.

If you or your child receives a message that is harassing, of a sexual nature, or threatening, forward a copy of the message to your online service provider and ask for their assistance.

The bottom line is that it's up to you, as parents, to set reasonable rules and guidelines for computer use by your children. Discuss these rules and post them near the computer as a reminder. Remember to monitor their compliance with these rules, especially when it comes to the amount of time your children spend on the computer. There is an Official Internet Contract on page 192 for this purpose.

You might consider keeping the computer in a family room rather than your child's bedroom. That way you all can share the experience of going online.

When you make using the Internet a family activity, you'll all enjoy the experience that much more.

Have fun surfing the Net,

CyberSarge

SAFE SURFING SOFTWARE

There are a number of programs out there that act as firewalls between the Internet and your children. There are two basic types of censorware, and they treat the problem in different ways:

1. **FILTER IT OUT.** Essentially these programs check Web pages for bad words. They allow access to the whole Internet, but block out sites that appear to contain potentially harmful content. The main drawback to this kind of system is that it is not really "smart" enough to analyze the total content, so it may block out a page that contains restricted words but that are being used in an otherwise non-threatening context. Or it may allow access to a Web site that has particularly violent content, but doesn't happen to use any of the restricted words.

2. **RATE IT.** These programs check Web sites for content ratings. Basically they allow limited access to the Internet—only to those Web sites that are within the rating categories you've approved for your kids. The major problem here is that the people operating the Web site have to decide their own rating categories. It's a kind of "rate yourself" environment.

To find more information on safe surfing, you should visit:

Who: THE SAFE SURF HOME PAGE
Where: *http://www.safesurf.com/*
What: This is an original Internet rating system dedicated to making the Internet safe for your children without censorship. They've developed and are implementing an Internet rating standard, bringing together parents, providers, publishers, developers, and all the resources available on the Internet to achieve this goal.

Who: THE RSAC

Where: *http://www.rsac.com/*

What: The Recreational Software Advisory Council is an independent organization that allows parents to evaluate Web sites by means of a ratings system. RSAC blocks unwanted content in four areas: language, nudity, sex, and violence. Right now it's set up to work automatically with only Microsoft's Internet Explorer. Parents can set up the browser to evaluate sites on any or all of the categories. Also many sites are displaying the RSAC logo to show that their content is safe for kids.

Who: CYBER PATROL

Where: *http://www.cyberpatrol.com*

What: Cyber Patrol lets you select twelve categories of adult material to control Web access. You can even block certain words and phrases in e-mail and chat rooms.

Who: CYBERSITTER

Where: *http://www.solidoak.com*

What: This software allows parents to view a list of their child's activities. Parents can restrict what phrases are sent and received and also block sites containing foul language.

Who: SURFWATCH

Where: *http://www.surfwatch.com*

What: This blocking software forbids access to discussion groups, chat rooms, and file libraries. It is possible to update blocked-site lists for a fee of sixty dollars per year.

OFFICIAL INTERNET CONTRACT

I, _____, Cyberspace Internaut, do solemnly swear

that I will surf the Net for no more than _____ hours a day or a total of

_____ hours per week.

I promise to keep my parents or teacher informed of all my activity
on the Internet.

I promise to obey CyberSarge's Top Ten Rules for Surfing the Net, including:

1. Never giving out personal information.

2. Avoiding unpleasant situations.

3. Always being myself.

4. Always keeping track of my time.

5. Always expressing myself but staying cool.

6. Always treating newbies as I would want to be treated.

7. Always using my common sense.

8. Always treating people online with respect.

9. Always sharing ideas, files, and helpful opinions.

10. Being an active and useful member of Cyberspace.

_____   _____

(signed) First Official Cyberspace Internaut   (date)

_____   _____

(signed) Grown-up   (date)

Chapter 10

Glossary:

More Technical (But Fun!) Terms You Might Come Across

Here's CyberSarge's dictionary of more cyberspeak terms so that you can talk the talk when you're on the Net. If you want to see where we talk about a word in context, you'll find other entries for it in the *Index of Terms*, starting on page 215.

Acronym

A shortcut in which a phrase is represented by its initials. For instance, FTP stands for File Transfer Protocol.

Address

An Internet address is just like your home or apartment address, only it is in cyberspace. Once you have an Internet address you have a place all your own on the Internet. All the Internet addresses given in this book are in ***bold italics*** to make sure the punctuation in them is not confused with regular punctuation. You do not need to use bold or italics when typing in any Internet addresses.

alt

This stands for alternative, one of the seven Usenet newsgroup categories.

American Standard Code for Information Interchange (ASCII)

ASCII text is plain, unformatted text that can be read by any computer's word processor.

Anonymous FTP

A way to download files from an FTP site when you are not registered at that site. Usually all you have to do is type in the word "anonymous" when asked for your log-in name to gain access to the site.

Applet

A tiny computer application, often used to describe Java programs. Web pages often have Java applets to animate scrolling text or provide music and sound effects.

Archie

An Internet service used for finding files from an FTP site.

Articles

Letters that are posted in newsgroups for all who subscribe to read. This is like a reporter writing an article for everyone who subscribes to the magazine.

Artificial reality

Similar to virtual reality, but more interactive, artificial reality lets the participant be part of, not just experience, the artificial environment. Often the user can even change the artificial environment.

Avatar

An on-screen digital "actor," often a chess piece or fish, used in Virtual Reality Markup Language (VRML) to stand in for a person on an online chat site, or playing a game.

Bandwidth

A way to measure the amount of data a network link can handle. For example, a modem with a baud rate of 14.4 has one-half the bandwidth of a 28.8 baud modem.

Baud

The speed at which modems transfer data. One baud is roughly equal to one bit per second.

Baud rate

A measurement of data transmission speed. Sometimes measured in bits per second. Your modem may have a baud rate of 14.4 Kbs, which is fourteen thousand, four hundred bits per second. (The capital K stands for a thousand.)

Binary

A method of counting often used in the world of computers, where all numbers are represented as combinations of 0 or 1.

Bit

The smallest unit of data that can be sent between computers. A bit is 0 or 1, off or on. Eight bits make a byte.

Bomb

A nasty piece of software that will cause a computer, or a network, to crash when it is run.

Bookmark

A small file, part of your Web browser, that keeps track of sites you've already visited and may want to revisit. Instead of having to retype the address, clicking on a bookmark will take you back there.

Boolean operator

The words "and," "or," and "not" are Boolean operators used to narrow down World Wide Web searches. For example, you can search for "computers NOT Apple."

Boot up

To turn on your computer.

Bounce

What your e-mail does when it cannot get to where you tried to send it. It either bounces back to you or goes off into deep cyberspace, never to be heard from again.

Browser

A Web browser is a software tool that lets you visit sites on the World Wide Web. (See also Web browsers.)

Bulletin board system

BBS is a network (not necessarily part of the Internet) that your computer can dial into with a modem. You communicate with other BBS users by exchanging messages and files. You can also download pictures that the bulletin board operator, or SYSOP, posts on the system for all users.

Byte

The number of bits needed to represent a letter (a,b,c) or number (1,2,3).

CD-ROM

This stands for "Compact Disk-Read Only Memory." The most popular high-capacity disk drive for computers, a CD-ROM drive can store over 600 megabytes of data.

Central Processing Unit

Also called a CPU, this is the main chip of a computer.

Chat

"Talking" with other people (usually by typing on your keyboard) over the Internet. Internet Relay Chat is the most often used method, but some World Wide Web sites offer chat capabilities. Chat stands for Conversational Hypertext Access Technology.

Chat groups

Online addresses where many people talk to each other at once.

Click on

This means you point at something on the screen with your mouse pointer—a picture or hypertext link—and click the mouse button.

Client

An Internet name for a computer that makes requests of another computer it's linked to, called a Server.

com

Short for commercial, com is one type of domain used in an Internet address (i.e. **IBM.com**). Other domains are edu, gov, org, and sci.

Comp

A newsgroup category concerned with computer issues.

Computer language

A system that allows different types of computers to speak to each other. Basically, computers translate English, or any other human language, into numbers because every computer can understand numbers.

Compression

A computer process for reducing the size of files to be sent over the Internet, in order to save on-line time. Two such compression methods are SIT and ZIP.

Computer Emergency Response Team

CERT is a security force for the Internet which maintains a clearinghouse for information about network security, including attempted—or successful—break-ins.

Cookies

Cookies are bits of text that a Web site leaves on your computer to track all kinds of information about your preferences.

Crackers

Computer experts who break into secure computer systems, often just for the sake of doing it.

Crash

When your computer gets confused by conflicting demands on it, it will shut down or refuse to do anything else until you reboot.

Cursor

The blinking line on a computer screen.

Cybercrime

The theft of data via computer by unauthorized users; all criminal activity in cyberspace.

Cyberian

An online librarian who makes a living doing information research and retrieval—a real hot "data surfer."

Cyberspace

That place where where people and computers meet. It is not a physical place, but another dimension reachable at your fingertips with your computer.

Datacops

Any agency that protects data. Most often it refers to the U.S. Secret Service.

Deck cowboys

Futuristic, some say fantasy, versions of a computer hacker or a modern-day cyberpunk.

Decompression

Returns compressed files to their natural size so that the information or data in the files can be used.

Delurking

When you come out of your shell and join the party online.

Desktop

The programs, represented by icons, that you keep on your computer screen. These may be your word processing files, your Internet provider, your Web browser, and whatever else you want direct access to.

Digital

Computers talk to other computers digitally. That is, they store and process information as a series of numbers (see Binary). Anything—including words, pictures, and sounds—can be "digitized" into the computer, then "undigitized" with a software program, like a word processor, so you can hear the sounds or see the pictures.

Digital cash

When you order something from a World Wide Web catalog, you use money that exists only in cyberspace.

Directory

The hard disk on your computer is divided into directories. Each directory can contain many different files. If you think of your hard disk as a file cabinet, then a directory is a drawer in that cabinet.

Discussion groups
People who get together on the Net to talk about a particular topic.

Disk drive
The part of your computer that transfers the information on your floppy disk into the computer's memory, or transfers what's in the computer's memory onto your hard disk. Think of this as a tape recorder that can play what is on the tape or can record music or words and put them on the tape. Disk drives come in two formats: a hard drive and a floppy drive.

Documents
They are more than just text. Think of computer documents as magazine articles or newspaper stories. Besides the words in the story, there may be pictures or maps or video clips to help you better understand the text.

Domain
The official name of a computer or service on the Internet. For example, the official e-mail address for the authors of this book is *kids@internet4kids.com*. The domain is *internet4kids.com*—everything after the @.

Dot
When you tell someone an Internet address, you say "kids at Internet 4 Kids DOT com." It looks like a period, but you call it a dot.

Down
When the network or your computer is not accessible, it's down.

Download
To transfer data from one computer to another. (See also Upload.)

Dweeb
A put-down describing someone who is really out of it.

Edu
This domain is for schools, universities, and other educational institutions.

E-mail
Electronic mail that you send to friends on other computers. It doesn't even need a postage stamp, and it gets there a lot faster than "snail mail."

Electronic mailbox
The place where your cyberspace mail goes to. Most Internet provider software includes e-mail capabilities, which will give you your own mailbox.

Escape character
A keyboard command that allows you to exit a computer system in case the system crashes or gets into a loop.

E-zine

Short for "electronic magazine." Sometimes e-zines have World Wide Web sites (like *Slate*, the biggest one); sometimes you get them delivered via e-mail.

FAQ

A Frequently Asked Question. The word most often describes a file of questions and answers about a particular subject. The file itself will often have *.faq* as part of its filename.

Feeb

A real incompetent at something, as in "I'm a real feeb when it comes to math."

Fiber-optic cable

The connection for much of cyberspace. Fiber-optic cable can carry much more data than a same-sized copper telephone cable.

File

A file is like a folder on your computer. It can contain text, pictures, or commands that make your computer perform some function, such as dialing up to an ISP or showing a picture.

File Transfer Protocol (FTP)

This is a method of sending and receiving files between computers over the Internet.

Filters

These are commands to software programs telling them to send data to a particular place so you don't have to do it by hand. Filters work just like coin sorters: Put any coin into the slot and the sorter directs the nickels to one slot, the dimes to another, and so on.

Firewall

An electronic barrier that keeps networks apart, or keeps unwanted data away.

Flame

To flame means to stomp on someone in cyberspace for saying something you consider wrong or just plain stupid, without being reasonable. It's kind of like slamming the door when you're mad.

Floppy disk

A flexible plastic disk that you insert into a computer's floppy disk drive to transfer or store information. These are also called diskettes.

Floppy drive

This is a disk drive that reads and writes from floppy disks. You stick a floppy disk into this drive.

Forum
In online services, a forum is a special place for discussing a certain subject.

Freenet
A bulletin board system that is connected to the Internet and is free of charge. Usually these are sponsored by community groups to give people free access to computing and information.

Freeware
This is software that you use and give to your friends without paying for it.

Garbage In, Garbage Out
Another phrase better known by its acronym, GIGO, this means that if you input sloppy data, you'll get back sloppy information.

Gateway
A gateway is a computer system that acts as a translator between different types of computers to allow them to interact in cyberspace.

Geeks
People who are really excited by computers and are proud of it.

Geek Speak
Using computer and Internet jargon when you talk or write. If you say, "I downloaded that way cool e-zine but it chewed up bandwidth," you're talking in geek speak.

Giga
A billion. As in a Gigabyte, a billion (1,000,000,000) bytes.

Gopher
A menu system that lets you to search for info on computers everywhere.

gov
Yet another domain name for government sites.

Graphic Interchange Format
Most often called by its acronym, GIF, this is a popular image file format on the Internet (See also JPEG.)

Graphics
Images and pictures.

Graphical User Interface
GUI, pronounced "gooey," is the method your computer's software uses to interact with you via the monitor. Pointing and clicking on icons is a typical Windows and Mac GUI.

Hacker
Someone who really knows how to navigate in cyberspace and can do neat

stuff like debug programs and fix computer problems. The term is often incorrectly used in a negative manner, but true Netizens know that the bad guys are called "crackers."

Handle

A nickname you pick for yourself, to be used when you're chatting and don't want to use your real name.

Handshake

This is what two modems do when they try to connect with one another in order to transfer data.

Hang

This is what happens when your computer fails to respond to mouse clicks or keystrokes.

Hard copy

A printout on paper of a computer document.

Hard disk

A metal platter coated with magnetic particles that is used to store data. A permanent part of your computer, hard disks can hold much more data and transfer that data at a higher speed than floppy disks.

Hard drive

The unit containing a hard disk and electronic instruments to read and write data.

Headers

Phrases at the start of a message that tell you what the message is about, as newspaper headlines tell you what the articles are about.

Helper applications

These applications are stand-alone programs that aren't a part of your Web browser. However, they can be downloaded to work within your browser.

Highlighted

When a word or a phrase is marked so that it stands out. The word might be in italics or bolded. On the Web highlighted words and phrases are hyperlinks that can take you to other locations.

Home page

The starting page of a World Wide Web site.

Host

A computer connected directly to the Internet. Like a restaurant host, who invites you into a restaurant and often seats you, a host computer acts as your gateway to the Internet.

Hotlist
Another name for a bookmark.

Hypermedia
This is hypertext with pictures and sounds, as well as words. Your computer might display images with sound or animated cartoons instead of text—all with pointers leading you to other locations where you'll find even more images, sound, and text!

Hypertext
One type of hypermedia, this is specially formatted text (it most often looks underlined or highlighted on the screen) used in World Wide Web documents. When you click on or choose this text, you will jump to the page that the hypertext is linked to. That new page will very likely have a hyperlink to take you to yet another World Wide Web page. You can travel all over the Web this way, and always jump back to where you began.

Hypertext Link
Addresses inserted into documents on the World Wide Web. Clicking on a link leads you to another document, another part of the same document, or an entirely different part of the Internet. (See also Hypertext.)

HyperText Markup Language (HTML)
Called HTML, this is the language of the World Wide Web, used to create all the Web pages you visit.

HyperText Transfer Protocol (HTTP)
Called HTTP, this is the method of communication between computers and networks on the Web.

Icon
A small image on the computer screen that executes a program or function when you point and click on it with your mouse. Icons are pictures that represent the program or function it executes.

Identity Hacking
The use of pseudo-anonymity or false accounts to pretend that one is another person on the Internet. Not nice.

Index file
A special file located in FTP directories. This is a list of what information is contained in each file on that particular computer. Think of an Index file like the index at the back of a book, telling you where in the book to go to find out about particular information.

Input/Output (I/O)

I/O is the way we communicate with computers, and the way they communicate with us. We type commands, or click with a mouse, and computers execute our instructions, and put images on the screen or make printouts.

Install

Setting up a software program so that it runs in your computer.

Installation program

A program that often comes with software to set it up on your computer. Sometimes it is called a setup program.

Integrated Services Digital Network (ISDN)

ISDN is a high-speed Internet connection, currently able to send and receive data at 126 Kilobytes per second (Kbps).

Interactive

This describes the two-way communication between computer programs and you and is often used to describe games where different input results in different outcomes.

Internauts

People who explore the new frontiers of cyberspace.

Internet

In the beginning there was the ARPANET, a wide area experimental network that linked universities and government research labs together. Over time, other groups formed their own networks. The collection of all these different networks linked together became what we now call the Internet.

Internet Relay Chat

Also called IRC, this is the first and still the most used method of chatting with others on the Internet. It requires a separate program to log on to computers called "chat servers," where you can join ongoing chats.

Internet service provider (ISP)

Your ISP is the company through which you connect to the Internet—unless you use an online service like the Microsoft Network or America Online.

Interzone

The wasteland setting of William Burroughs's 1959 novel, *Naked Lunch*, the Interzone has become a favorite haunt for cyberpunk writers.

Java

A computer language used on the World Wide Web that works with your browser to produce sounds and animated images on Web sites.

Java-enhanced site

A site that has Java programs to run animation. A minimum of 16 megabytes of RAM is necessary to run Java programs, and your browser should be a 3.0 version or higher.

JPEG

Another image type used on the Internet. (See also Graphic Interchange Format or GIF.)

Key

In computerese, a key is often a way to "unlock" or install a software program. It is a form of copy protection.

Key pal

Key pals are pen pals that you communicate with through the computer. Since you use a keyboard to type your e-mail letters, pen pals in cyberspace are called key pals.

Key word

A password that opens up the doors of the World Wide Web. Typing in the words "baseball," "pitcher," and "World Series" will help you find documents containing all of those words.

Kludge

Nontraditional ways to fix computer problems that aren't in any manual, such as using chewing gum to hold down a faulty microchip, or linking together two poorly written computer programs to get a result that one well-written program could do.

Listserver

A special type of program that handles e-mail among subscribers to a list or discussion group.

Listserver mailing list

A subscription list of the members of a particular discussion group. When you join, or subscribe to, a list, you get all the e-mail addressed to that list from all its members. When you post a message to that list, all the members will read what you've written.

Log off

To sign off or disconnect from a remote computer.

Log on, or log in

What you do when you connect to a remote computer.

Loop

A faulty instruction to a computer may cause it to repeat the same command over and over again, sometimes causing the computer to crash, or freeze.

Lurking

Hanging around in the background and watching without getting involved. Most of us are lurkers when we first enter a new neighborhood on the Internet.

Mailing list

See Listserver mailing list.

Metasearch site

A World Wide Web search tool that uses other search tools to answer a query.

Megahertz (MHz)

Mega means million; hertz is one cycle per second of an electronic wave; so one Megahertz is one million cycles per second.

Misc

Short for "miscellaneous." Another of the seven Usenet newsgroup categories, this one is made up of groups that don't fit into the other six.

Modem

This stands for "modulator-demodulator." It's a device that allows your computer to link up with other computers over telephone lines.

Mouse

A hand-held pointing device used to move the cursor around the computer screen. A mouse has one, two, or more buttons to execute commands, such as clicking on icons. Other pointing devices are trackballs, joysticks, and touch pads.

MUD

An acronym for Multi-User Dimension (or Dungeon or Domain), MUDs are multi-user role-playing games that exist on the Internet for entertainment purposes. MUDs are mostly text-based virtual worlds which many players (participants) may explore, change, or add on to. In most cases, the MUD is actually a game with scores, player attributes, levels, etc., but some MUDs have educational or social goals in mind. Game-oriented MUDs are usually based on different science fiction genres such as fantasy, space, or even cyberpunk. Other types are called MOOs— for MUD object-oriented—which give the player more control over his or her environment.

Multimedia

The combination of images, sound, and motion, which is built into many of today's computer games. Most often found on CD-ROMs, multimedia games are beginning to be seen on the World Wide Web.

Multipurpose Internet Mail Extensions
Also called MIME, this is the Internet protocol for sending and receiving e-mail.

National Center for Supercomputing Applications (NCSA)
The NCSA is a research center on the University of Illinois campus. Mosaic, the first Web browser, was developed here.

Nanosecond
One billionth of a second. Some things in cyberspace happen this fast.

National Science Foundation (NSF)
The NSF funds NSFNet, a high-speed network that once formed the backbone of the Internet in the United States.

Nerd
If you spend way too much time at your computer, are able to fix problems on other people's computers, and use a lot of geek speak, people will think you're a computer nerd. That's okay; just remind them that billionaire Bill Gates, owner of Microsoft, is a nerd.

Net
Sometimes written as net, it's short for Internet.

Net surfing
Visiting sites on the World Wide Web. Also called browsing or cruising.

Netiquette
The proper way to behave when you're surfing the Internet, such as respecting the rights and opinions of others and treating others the way you want to be treated. (See also Flame.)

Netizen
A combination of the words "network" and "citizen" or "denizen." A person who spends time in cyberspace, using netiquette.

Network
A group of computers joined by data-carrying links. A network may be as small as two or three personal computers tied together by local telephone lines in the same building, or it may be a vast complex of computers spread across the world, whose data links include telephone lines, satellite relays, fiber-optic cables, or radio links.

Network News Transfer Protocol (NNTP)
NNTP is the method by which news servers talk to one another.

Newbie

This is what we were called when we were new at this Internet thing.

Newsreader software programs

Programs that usually come with your Internet service software and allow you to read the news available in newsgroups.

Newsgroups

Online gatherings devoted to many topics of discussion, from how to train your pet to the latest UFO rumors. (See also Usenet.)

Offline

When you're not connected to another computer system.

Ohnosecond

That terrible moment in time when you realize you've just made a BIG mistake—like erasing all the files in the wrong subdirectory.

Online

When you are connected to another computer system.

org

Short for organization, this domain category most often represents non-profit organizations, such as National Public Radio, at *NPR.org*.

Packet

A unit of Internet communication; a chunk of data. When you send an e-mail or a file over the Internet, it is broken down into packets when it is sent, and then regrouped at the other end when it is received.

Password

A secret name that you and only you know. Online services such as America Online, and your Internet service provider require you to use a password when you log on to their servers.

Paste

Clipping sections from one file and putting them into another.

Peripheral

An extra device, like a modem or printer, you can attach to your computer.

PING

A program that can trace the route a message takes from your computer through the Internet to another computer.

Plug-In

An add-on program for Web browsers to increase their usefulness. Some plug-ins allow sound to be played when you link to a Web page; other plug-ins run video images.

Point-to-Point Protocol (PPP)

PPP is the way your computer talks to a computer that's connected to the Internet. (See also Serial Line Interface Protocol.)

Port

This is the plug at the back of your computer where you can attach a modem, a printer, or a mouse. A port is a number that identifies a particular Internet service (for instance, Port 6667 usually means an IRC server.)

Post Office Protocol (POP)

POP is the system that allows Internet mail servers to act just like a real post office. A POP server looks at the mail that arrives, and then sends it on to its final destination.

Posting

Entering messages to a newsgroup.

Pretty Good Privacy (PGP)

An encryption, or coding program that prevents anyone but you from reading your e-mail.

Program

A set of instructions for computers.

Prompt

When your computer asks you to do something and waits for you to respond. For example, if you see the phrase *login*: or *logon*:, the computer is waiting for you to type in your user name.

Protocol

A set of rules for computers to talk to one another over a network.

Public domain

When a program is put into the public domain, anyone may download it and use it free of charge.

Query

A question for a search site, often written in key words. Typing in "automobiles AND Chrysler" at a search site is a query. It's like saying, "Go out on to the Web and find me documents dealing with Chrysler automobiles."

QuickTime

An Apple plug-in that allows videos to run within your browser.

Random access memory

RAM, in the form of microchips on a plug-in circuit board, can be added to most computers to increase their ability to carry out instructions. Any data in RAM is lost when you turn off your computer. For example, when someone says, "I've got 16 megabytes of RAM in my computer," they are referring to this type of memory.

Readme files

Text files often found on FTP sites, or included with software, that tell the user something about the site or the program.

Read-only memory (ROM)

ROM contains the basic information a computer needs to boot up when you turn on the power switch. ROM memory holds its data even when the computer is off.

Real time

The actual time of an event. An e-mail from your friend was written in the past. But when you join a chat group, you can read messages from your friend as they are typed, or in real time.

rec

A Usenet category devoted to recreational and sports activities.

Remote computer

Another computer connected to your computer via telephone lines (or other network connections).

sci

The domain of science organizations.

Script

A series of instructions, often written in text form, for a computer to execute. For example you can write a script instructing your computer to log on to the atomic clock site in Colorado every Sunday morning and set your computer's clock.

Scrolling

Using the mouse or arrow keys located at the side of your screen to move the screen up, down, or sideways.

Search engine

A program designed to explore the Internet to look for specific information. A search engine is like a librarian who looks for the books in the library that you request.

Search site

A Web site with a search engine, or with a database containing information about what's on the Internet.

Search words

See key words.

Serendipity

Discovering things by accident, often while looking for something else.

Serial Line Interface Protocol (SLIP)

SLIP is another way computers talk to Internet servers. (See also PPP.)

Server

A computer that provides a particular service over the Internet, such as mail, chat, or FTP.

Service provider

An organization, such as America Online, or NetCom, that provides access to the Internet.

Set up

Installing a software program on your computer.

Shareware

Shareware doesn't cost you anything to get and try out. If you like it and want to use it, then the author of the program asks for a small licensing fee. (See also Freeware.)

Shortcut

Used in Windows 95, a shortcut is an icon, representing a file or program, that you click on to open. You create your own shortcuts by dragging and dropping an icon onto your desktop.

Signal-to-noise ratio

This phrase has a technical meaning, but you're most likely to hear it used as an unflattering way to compare the useful discussion in a newsgroup (signal) with the mindless chatter (noise). A low signal-to-noise ratio means lots of bandwidth-wasting chitchat, and not much good stuff.

Signature file

A file created in your word processor that is attached to every e-mail that you send.

Simple Mail Transfer Protocol (SMTP)

SMTP is the language Internet mail servers use to talk to one another and to exchange e-mail letters.

Site

Refers to the physical location of a computer. The word is sometimes used to refer to where a computer is located in cyberspace as well. For instance, when you go to MyNet's site, you are going (either through the Internet, or physically by walking or taking a bus) to the place where the MyNet computer exists.

Smiley

When you're face-to-face, you can smile, frown, or do a multitude of facial expressions to enhance your words. You can also sound happy, sad, angry, or just plain bored. In e-mail your words have to carry your thoughts by themselves, so folks invented smileys to punctuate their phrases. They are also called "emoticons" (for "emotion" and "icon"). There are two basic types of smileys: those with words and those with pictures.

Snail mail

The good old U.S. Postal Service, where letters may take days to reach their recipients, as compared to the instant transmission of e-mail.

soc

Another Usenet category dealing with social and political issues.

Software

Anything that helps the computer, or hardware, to carry out tasks. (See also Program.)

SPAM

Sending Particularly Annoying Messages. SPAM is most often advertising. If you ever receive a message advertising a "fantastic business opportunity" from someone you've never heard of, this is SPAM.

Spamming

The act of sending unwanted e-mail, often to Usenet newsgroups that have no relation to the message topic. Most Netizens consider this rude, and often send a request to the originator of the message, asking him or her to stop.

Streaming audio

Lets you hear digitized sound as it is being broadcast over the Net.

Supercomputer

A mainframe-sized computer that operates much faster than a normal desktop or laptop computer, and is used for special science and military projects.

Surfing

Traveling through cyberspace via your computer.

SYSOP

Sysop is the System Operator. Someone who runs a computer system or bulletin board.

Transmission Control Protocol/Internet Protocol (TCP/IP)

The set of communication rules developed by the University of California for the Department of Defense.

Telephony

The combination of the Internet with the telephone, which allows the ability to talk long distances over the Internet. This is like a personal phone call, but you use the computer.

Telnet

The network terminal protocol that allows you to log on to any other computer on the network anywhere in the world. At Telnet sites, you can only access the information that the site allows you to, unless you already have an account; often university networks work this way, allowing you to access their library information.

Text

Text simply means words.

Threads

In a discussion group, a thread is simply the topic of a particular series of messages. You can subscribe to digests of many newsgroups that only list the topic threads, so you can read the messages you're interested in, and skip the others.

Transfer mode

FTP requires you to tell both your computer and the host computer the kind of file you're uploading or downloading. Binary is used for programs, graphics, and sound files; ASCII for plain text files.

Twit filter

A routine in most e-mail programs that allows you to ignore messages from somebody you don't want to hear from. (See also Filter.)

Universal Resource Locator (URL)

Some folks say "earl," some say "yew-are-ell," but they both mean URL, the addresses for any resource on the World Wide Web. Some URLs are FTP sites, some Gopher servers, some a single file residing on the same site. When you find a hypertext link, it's usually related to an URL.

UNIX

A computer operating system developed at Bell Labs in the early 1970s, UNIX is the dominant operating system on the Internet.

Upload
Sending information or files from your computer to another computer, usually through a modem.

Usenet newsgroups
A collection of newsgroups that are devoted to particular interests of a group of people. Newsgroups might discuss the environment or the latest movie gossip. There are over 20,000 Usenet newsgroups covering almost any topic you can imagine. If you can't find one on a topic you want to discuss, you can start your own newsgroup.

User ID
Also called user name, this is how you identify yourself to your online service or ISP. This is not the same as your password.

Utility programs
Special programs to help you keep your computer running the way you want it to.

Voice modem
A modem that comes equipped with a microphone attached in order to hear and transmit sound.

Virtual community
Any group or gathering that exists in cyberspace. It might be a BBS, a hacking group, a network, or even a zaibatsu.

Virtual reality
VR is a world that exists only in cyberspace. Modern-day virtual reality uses helmets, gloves, and bodysuits connected to computers that allow you to experience computer-generated sensations. Once "jacked in" (a William Gibson phrase) you can walk around three-dimensional objects, move things, and communicate with other VR users. A goal of some virtual reality researchers is to generate a completely alternate reality. The possibilities of VR-generated environments are as limitless as the imagination.

Virtual Reality Markup Language (VRML)
A programming language used to build interactive games on the Internet.

Virtual tourist
A visitor in cyberspace; a bit like lurking on a newsgroup.

Virus
A computer bug that infects whole systems and networks, created by crackers.

Web browsers

Programs that let you navigate through the World Wide Web and see graphics and text on your computer screen. They also allow you to make hypertext leaps to other Web sites. There are many Web browser programs, such as Netscape Navigator and Microsoft Explorer. When you sign up to go online, the company you sign up with will usually send a Web browser software program to get you started.

Web server

A computer attached to a network that is used for communication with the World Wide Web.

Web site

A place on the World Wide Web that has a unique address. A Web site will have a home page and sometimes have many other pages linked to that page.

What You See Is What You Get

WYSIWYG, pronounced "wizzywig," is a computer program's ability to print out on paper (hard copy) exactly what is on the screen.

Wildcard

If you want to search the World Wide Web for subjects like automaton, automate, and semi-automatic, type *auto* as your key word. Asterisks make your search word a wildcard.

Worm

A computer virus that can replicate itself. In 1987, the "Internet Worm" shut down hundreds of computers worldwide.

World Wide Web (WWW or the Web)

The most popular and fastest-growing part of the Internet. It's got pictures and hypertext, which means you can jump from one place to another, all over the world, with a single click of a mouse.

Yahoo

A search engine that helps you find information on the Internet.

Zaibatsu

A Japanese term used a lot by the cyberspace writer William Gibson, which means a large mega-corporation, such as Sony.

Index of Terms

ABOUT THE AUTHORS

Ted Pedersen has been involved with computers since his days as a programmer in Seattle. A freelance writer for the past 15 years, with more than 100 animated TV credits, Ted continues to work as a computer consultant and more recently was a content creator for the World Wide Web. He has written *The Tale of the Virtual Nightmare* for Nickelodeon's *Are You Afraid of the Dark?* book series, and four *Star Trek: Deep Space Nine* young adult novels. Ted and his wife, Phyllis, share their Venice, California, home with several cats and computers.

Francis Moss has written more than 150 animated TV scripts and has been story editor on the "Teenage Mutant Ninja Turtles" and "James Bond, Jr." television shows. He was a contributing author on *Using Windows 95, Special Edition,* and his nonfiction children's book, *Grizzly!,* will be published in 1998. A computer consultant, he has been actively surfing the Internet for years and often beta tests new software, particularly Microsoft Windows 95 and 98. Francis and his wife, Phyllis, live in North Hollywood, California, with their two children, Zachary and Caitlin, one dog, two cats, and three computers.

NOTES